"A gorgeous meditation on pain and destruction, reclamation and regrowth. This lush, magical story of heart-break, healing, and hope in the aftermath is a balm to the soul. Perfect for fans of Becky Chambers and Premee Mohamed."

—Kelsea Yu, Shirley Jackson award-nominated author of *Bound Feet* and *Demon Song*

"Luscombe and Stock conflate the best and worst of humanity in this tender, creative, and thoughtful meditation on the destruction we've wrought on our world—and what it demands in return. Featuring lovable characters and a fascinating characterization of Earth that bleeds through every word, *Human Scars on Planet Skin* is a necessary addition to climate fiction."

—S. Hati, author of *And the Sky Bled*

"In *Human Scars on Planet Skin*, Effie Joe Stock and Nathaniel Luscombe create a unique and often terrifying world. This impressive psychedelic trip blends body horror, eco fiction, and lyrical prose to create a brutal, unflinching, and mesmerizing reading experience."

—A. D. Sui, author of *The Dragonfly Gambit*

"Brimming with emotion, haunting in its symbolism, and unapologetically unique, this is the book I didn't know I was looking for. Human Scars on Planet Skin meets you at the intersection of environmental devastation, overwhelming grief, and dogged restoration. It's a story of the scars of both the world and those we carry with us. Of the things we cannot carry. Of our place in the balance of nature, life, death, and the other souls around us. Of the pain and process of healing, even in the face of unspeakable horror. This is a one-of-a-kind story for those looking for a visceral, heart-felt journey that takes you to the depths of despair while also high-lighting the tenacity of hope."

—Hayley Reese Chow, author of *Into the Churn*

"Human Scars on Planet Skin tenderly explores non-human perspectives as it takes the reader on a journey through a human-ravaged world. Unique and unafraid to hold humankind accountable for its actions, this book is what modern sci-fi should be doing more of."

—Drew Huff, author of *Landlocked in Foreign Skin*

HUMAN SCARS
ON
PLANET SKIN

HUMAN SCARS ON PLANET SKIN
A Science Fantasy Horror Novel

Paperback ISBN: 978-1-962337-26-7
Ebook ISBN: 978-1-962337-27-4
Hardback ISBN: 978-1-962337-28-1

Published in Hackett, AR, USA by Dragon Bone Publishing™ 2025.

Cover design and illustrations are created by and copyright of Effie Joe Stock. Interior formatting by Effie Joe Stock. Edited by Samantha Mendell.

I, Effie Joe Stock, dedicate this book to Mother Earth and my own Mother,—the two creatures brave enough to hold me and all my emotions and never judge me once.

&

I, Nathaniel Luscombe, dedicate this to those who feel more at home in their body as they get older. I hope this book takes you by the hand and helps you heal. I know that writing it healed me.

TRIGGER WARNINGS:

Body Horror & Dysmorphia

Plant & Environmental Horror

Dissociation

Grief and Trauma Surrounding Death

Frightening Imagery

Scenes Involving Decay & Corpses

Colonization

HUMAN SCARS ON PLANET SKIN

EFFIE JOE STOCK

NATHANIEL LUSCOMBE

FOREWORD

This is a book about a planet reclaiming her skin from those who wish to tame it, chain it, cultivate it. This is a book about a shroomperson who can't help but lie to themself to cover up the death around them, to cover up the death inside them growing from places they've buried out of self-hatred and shame. This is a book about creatures so wrapped up in saving the world, they forget to save themselves. This is a book about the horrors lying just under the skin, waiting until one sinks, alone, into the depths of their soul before writhing free and setting loose a darkness one thinks may never end.

Except, this isn't really a book about . . . any of those things.

Because it's a book about you. It's a book about me. And I think, somewhere between its pages and the folds and tears in our own skin, that is where fiction ends and the real horror begins.

I hope it holds you the same way it held me, fitting broken pieces together not to create something whole, functional, or appealing, but rather something beautiful, something worthy of existence and love just because it *survived*.

Because if that is enough for a little shroomperson and a sentient planet, then it's enough for you. And it's enough for me.

—*Effie Joe Stock*

PLAYLIST

"**Dying Star**" — *Ashnikko, Ethel Cain*

"**If the World Falls to Pieces**" — *Young Summer*

"**Creatura**" — *HANA*

"**Melancholy**" — *Gustixa*

"**Fruits of the Dark**" — *Dune Moss*

"**Just Be**" — *Jamie Grace*

"**The Seed**" — *AURORA*

"**The Wolves**" — *Cyrus Reynolds, Keeley Bumford*

"**I Saw The Mountains**" — *Noah Cyrus*

"**Tell it to My Heart**" — *Paris Paloma*

"**Pull Down**" — *Evy Frearson*

"**Plant People**" — *Ben Salisbury, Geoff Barrow*

"**endless**" — *Oklou*

"**Somewhere Only We Knew**" — *Gustixa, rhianne*

"**PISCES (falling up)**" — *kate the dreamer*

"**What Was I Made For**" — *Billie Eilish*

"Heartbeat" — *Ghostly Kisses*

"Shadow of Mine" — *Alec Benjamin*

"IM SORRY" — *MARO, NASAYA*

"Imagination" — *Juniper Vale, RØRE*

"I Am My Own" — *Dune Moss*

"Daniel" — *Aidoneus*

Listen to the full playlist on Spotify:

HUMAN SCARS ON
PLANET SKIN

by Effie Joe Stock, and Nathaniel Luscombe

GLOSSARY

Apis Turrian — A sentient honeybee responsible for herding non-sentient honeybees; a shepherd honeybee

Dama — Parental title shroombabies call their shroomparents

Headcap/shroomcap — the dome-like shroompeoples' heads, sometimes where spores are released

Isagani — Turr's largest garden city; a harmonious, cultivated ecosystem many Turrians call home

Nyphern — a spiny leafed vine with paralyzing properties for self defence

Shroomperson — Any sentient mushroom

Turrian — Any sentient plant or insect living on Turr

Unique Life — The life force gifted to non-sentient plants and insects that cause them to become sentient

TURR
ISAGANI
DAFFODIL TREES
SHROOM CAVES
FUNGUS FOREST
LILY P
TOWN
RESLEY'S
VINE GARDEN

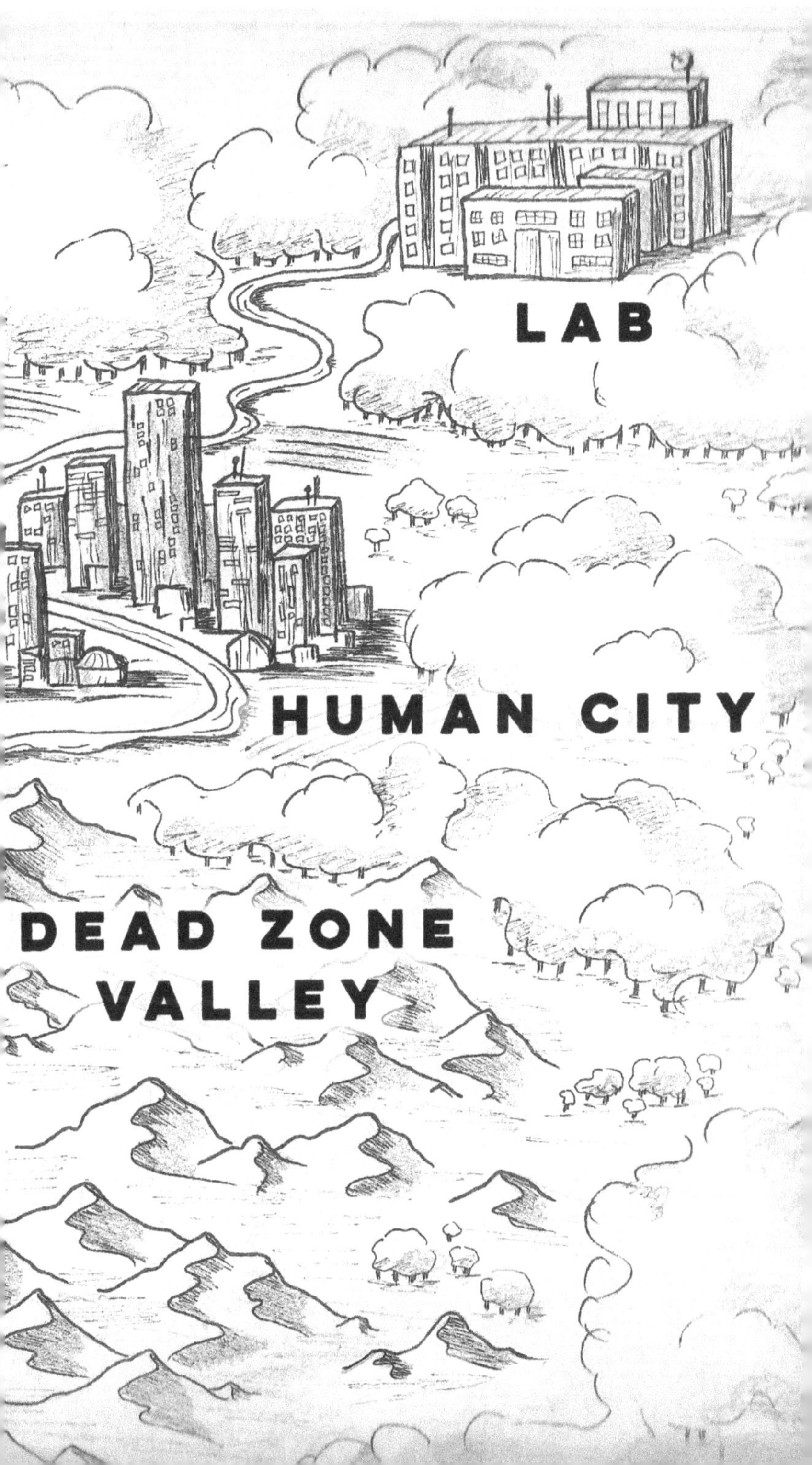

LAB
HUMAN CITY
DEAD ZONE VALLEY

TURR

Day 0 Since the Humans' Exodus from Turr's Skin

Pain radiated through Turr's bones. She'd been holding herself back for some time, building the energy and courage for what she was about to do. No longer could she watch as the humans tore apart the ecosystems on her body. They were parasites and they'd long overstayed their welcome.

Her vengeance started as a gentle quake running across her surface.

The light of her sun rose and warmed the places the humans lived. Places that should belong to Turr's people. Though once wild, tuned to the gentle song of life Turr used to sing, they now lay tamed and cultivated for an unfamiliar, unyielding sort of civilization. Twisted forms of technology forced life from the soil, giving nothing in return. Tall structures rose unnaturally, housing the humans. The exposed ground around their buildings burned from carelessly discarded toxins.

Turr stretched within her form, testing the limits

of her strength for the first time in years, a quake rippling along her surface. Though her children had taken her silence as a surrender, she'd rather die than submit herself beneath the hands of these aliens. She'd spent time gathering strength and learning about their systems. Now she knew how their world worked. Now she knew where to attack.

A second, stronger quake rippled through her bones, a full-body movement to assure herself of her capabilities. The threads of life snapped taut. She counted them—fewer than there used to be.

With a surge of anger, she pushed herself into the plants and began her attack.

The first buildings to fall under her wrath peeled back like a lifeless scab. The only plants that responded to her soul were the ones growing along the city outskirts. She overextended herself, pushing the thick vines beyond their limits to crawl across dead soil and wrap themselves around the human structures. Structures she'd grown used to, grown around, were now torn from her skin, leaving pockmarks in their wake where she'd forgotten to live.

This first attack gave her more strength. She took back more of her land, the forests growing and expanding, taking on a life of their own as she gave them strength to fight.

When her limbs found one of her own creatures, she wrapped them with life to protect them from her rage. When she found humans, she ripped them apart and consumed their flesh, using the life they'd stolen to fuel herself.

With the fear of Turr's raging soul burned deep into their own bones, the humans prepared to flee. The angry planet, once so lush, now grew vengeful and thirsty for blood.

Screams rippled the air. Death permeated the once clean atmosphere. Desperate for materialistic wealth even at the expense of their lives, the humans gathered their belongings, riches and trinkets they thought they couldn't live without and ran from their houses—buildings they'd borrowed from Turr's bones and never thought to return.

The humans' ships had lay dormant for five years, stilled in their assurance that Turr was their new home. But this unexpected eviction changed everything. They engaged the jets of their massive ships. Turr had grown over them through the years, thin layers of plant life spreading across the metal. When the jets engaged, the heat grew unbearable, and the plants curled back, dying.

Turr felt this death and wept.

Fire poured from the ships, singeing the plants, roasting fungus trees, and charring daffodil forests. Turr writhed within her melting form. It'd been years since she'd first felt this scale of destruction. It would take years more to recover.

But what was extra recovery? She was already a damaged thing, already clinging to life with everything she had. She would rather push herself to the brink of death and be free than remain alive in this state.

Some of the ships rose into the air, then fell back down as the engines died, old fuel betraying them. Explosions bloomed across Turr's skin. Plants withered and burned. Turr's children died. Other ships pushed onward, rising into the atmosphere.

Turr groaned as her plants receded from the city. She no longer had the strength to continue her attack. Even amidst the burning, relief coursed through her as the weight of the ships left her form. The human's reign over her had ended.

Or so she thought.

With a last spurt of technological horror, the human ships jumped into hyperdrive, dumping thousands of gallons of toxins into the sky.

Turr screamed and shook, tearing her bones and skin apart with violent quakes, straining away from the toxins. But her atmosphere trapped and spread them. Her gravity brought them closer. She could do no more to protect herself or her children.

The toxins settled.

They burned, seeping into her, melting away an entire region. The thriving life there curled in on itself, transforming into rot. No life could flourish within this bubble of death. Color drained from lifeless bodies, leaving behind an aching void.

Turr opened her skies and cried. The rain, cold where it used to be warm, struggled to wipe clean the blackened forests—shells of the beautiful life that once lived on and decorated Turr's skin.

Her efforts were not enough. The toxins had settled deep. Like all things, they had roots—dark, torturous roots that knew no boundaries. Poison entered Turr's veins.

The land, which once sung with life, fell silent.

Turr had wanted the humans to leave for so long. Ever since they stepped their small feet onto her skin, they'd done nothing but leave footprints of incomprehensible destruction. But would she have forced them so quickly from the planet they'd tried desperately to tame, to cultivate, to oppress, had she known the damage they'd leave in their wake? Even as the humans fled back between the stars, they left behind deep scars that might never fade.

She ached to lay down and rest, to succumb to the painful silence spreading across her. Instead, she stirred once more.

Through waves of grassy expanse, moss under dandelion forests, purple waters holding lily pad towns, she reached and searched for any last living souls on her surface.

> *Find each other and you will find me.*
> *Through each other's eyes you will learn to see.*
> *The answers I will give you through memories.*
> *Then in healing yourselves, you will heal me.*

INVIDIA

Day 0 Since Humans Made the Dead Zones

Bright sunlight brushed against the shroomperson's soft, rubbery skin like an old lover. Turning their pudgy face to the roof of their cave, Invidia smiled, letting the morning air soak into their body, their cells, then down into the ground under their feet where their roots had stretched and grown overnight.

A quick glance at the compost floor of their cave filled them with pride. Dozens of little mushrooms had sprouted from the moist soil—stems plump and healthy, caps shining pink with sparkling white ridges. Bending down, Invidia trailed their fingers across the mushrooms' caps.

"Maybe one day, Turr will bless one of you with the unique life, and I'll have a little shroombaby of my own." A smile spread across their face. Desperately, they yearned to make such a contribution to the thriving ecosystem of Turr's sentient plants and pollinators. Full of hope, they gently broke their thick feet from the soil and roots below. Unlike sentient shroombabies, this common fungi growth no longer needed a parent's support.

Invidia gingerly stepped across the fungus circle. Trying to hide their bright smile, they collected a few of the mushrooms before stashing them away in a leafy bag. They pushed through a thick growth of pink shimmering vines covering the cave entrance and stepped into the bustling garden city of Isagani.

Immediately, the bustle of Turr's largest ecological city bombarded Invidia. Dozens of creatures ran or flew back and forth, tending to the vast gardens, their sole purpose on Turr to take care of her plants and creatures. To become sentient, to take upon the responsibility of maintaining such a vibrant, thriving ecosystem, was a Turrian's highest calling.

"If you take care of Turr," Invidia sang as another shroomperson pushed out of their own cave, stretching their thin yellow legs.

"She will take care of you!" the neighboring shroomperson finished with a wink, tipping the corner of their orange and yellow spotted headcap. A sprinkling of orange spores scattered on the ground as they laughed, waving to their friend. Invidia waved back enthusiastically as their neighbor picked up a reed pail, ready to gather more compost.

All Turrians lived by those words: Take care of the planet and she will take care of you. Invidia's eyes strayed over the large fungus forest, across the tops of the daffodil trees beyond, and finally to the human mega city. Its metal buildings and glass windows stood in stark contrast to the ecological surface of Turr. The humans, who'd arrived years before, didn't know these words of the land. Instead of caring for Turr, they'd come to take, steal, and corrupt.

"We'll never be safe until they're gone." The memory of their friend's words echoed through their mind. Balling their stem-like hands into fists, Invidia forced themself to look at the human's city. If Turr herself couldn't hide her face from the abomination, neither should they.

The last few months had been the worst. The entire might of Isagani had nearly reached its limit fending off the spreading illnesses brought upon them by the humans. The destruction had become impossible to ignore as once purple waters turned indigo, then brownish blue. The plants closest to the humans were shrinking. An entire fungus and daffodil forest near the metropolis had been reduced to a field of dirt where the humans planted their own strange crops—crops that stole from the soil rather than gave back to it.

"You're not a fighter type." Invidia's hands painfully clutched their bag as the memory's familiar words

rattled in their mind. *"Even among the gentle types you're the weakest. Shroompeople aren't meant for fighting or protecting. They're not even meant to be out in the storms or the sun."*

But Invidia refused to be confined to the dark crevasse of their cave. Though they desired more than anything to raise their own shroombabies, to be satisfied with the familiar life of collecting and digesting compost like the other shroompeople, they couldn't help the urge to rebel. They felt called to do something *more*. To heal Turr so their future shroombabies could thrive, not just survive.

So instead of grabbing their own reed pail and following the slow march of colorful shroompeople to the compost collection, Invidia pressed their leafy bag of shrooms tighter to their chest and ducked down the road in the opposite direction.

"Invidia!" a trilling voice called out behind them, accompanied by the low humming of wings.

Wincing, Invidia turned and waved at the wasp creature hovering a few feet off the ground. "Hello, Lorna!"

"Where are you going?" Lorna asked, eying the unusual bag. "I thought we were going to watch the butterflies today? And why aren't you going to the compost collection?"

Invidia's cream-colored cheeks darkened to match their headcap, their mouth running dry. "Oh! I'm so sorry. I completely forgot." They wanted to bury themselves in their cave again, shame eating at them like a beetle.

Lorna sighed, her little antenna bobbing as she planted two of her spindly legs on her thorax. "You always forget, Invidia." Her buzzing words sounded forgiving, but her eyes shone with disappointment. "You forgot last time too."

With shaking hands, Invidia reached into their bag and pulled out three shrooms. "I know, I'm so sorry. I'm not very good with . . . time." But really, they weren't very good with anything that didn't include ideas to get rid of the humans. "Here, take a few. I know they can't do much to . . . fix anything"—they sighed bitterly—"but perhaps they can help you forget the pain for a while." Invidia handed the psychedelic mushrooms to Lorna who took them with a small, sad smile.

When the humans first arrived, Lorna's family had marched off to fight them. They'd never returned. Since then, her friendship with Invidia had become strained. Lorna reached out for companionship, and Invidia withdrew, unsure how to comfort against the pain of death.

"Thank you, Invidia. I appreciate it."

But her kind words didn't convince Invidia. In fact, they felt certain Lorna's pity was directed more toward themself rather than her own tragedy. Discomfort twisting painfully inside them, Invidia refused to meet Lorna's gaze until she pointed to their bag.

"So, where are you off to today?"

A thousand excuses raced through Invidia's mind. Finally, they settled on a half truth. As a psychedelic shroom type, lies always came more easily. "Resley has some new vine sprouts that I'm supposed to gather for the regrowth team. They want to plant them around Isagani to fill the wall's gaps."

Lorna buzzed an unsure tone. "Is that *all*?"

Invidia nodded a bit too fast, too aggressively. They both knew runs for new seedlings were done once a week—one having been conducted just yesterday—and never by a shroomperson.

Lorna searched Invidia's face, looking as if she would ask another question, but Invidia didn't let her.

"I'm sorry for forgetting our butterfly watching date. Perhaps we can try again next week?" They turned away, effectively closing the conversation.

A sparkle formed in Lorna's eyes as they forced a smile and nodded. "Of course. Absolutely."

They both knew it was a lie.

Lorna didn't stop Invidia as they turned away and started back down the road. Though their plan had worked, something inside them almost wished it hadn't.

It took Invidia nearly the entire morning to reach Isagani's outskirts where their friend Resley grew his vines. He loved growing them in little mazes, joking that all the pathways led to the center so he could always find his way back home. The towering growths of vines stretched for miles, doubling as the outer walls of Isagani, separating the cultivated land of the garden city from the wilderness beyond.

"Hello, Resley! I'm here!" Invidia jumped up and down, peering through enormous leaves, straining to catch a glimpse of their tall, green-skinned friend.

"Invidia! You're earlier than I expected. Did you bring a wet bag?" Resley ducked under the heart-shaped leaf he'd been attending to and strode over to Invidia. Young vines reached out to him like children seeking attention from a loving parent.

Invidia patted the bag proudly. "I did. I'll make sure to wet it again on the trip back." They rummaged through the bag before pulling out the rest of the mushrooms. "And I brought some shrooms for you as well."

A smile spread across his leafy lips as he brushed hair-like vines from his face, tucking them behind his ears. "You know you didn't have to do that."

Invidia bowed, their pink cap bobbing vigorously. "Of course I did. I have my own shroom growth back at my cave. I have plenty to hand out now."

"Your own growth! Does that mean you'll grow other shroompeople?"

A bright smile lit their face as their stomach fluttered. "I hope so. Most of my friends are already Damas to their own shroombabies." They signed deeply, lowering their shoulders. "But I don't know if it'll even happen. I haven't been spending as much time around the mushroom caves and compost gardens as I should and now I feel behind, and—"

Resley placed his hand on Invidia's shoulder. Little vines stretched from his green fingertips as he gave a reassuring squeeze. "Don't worry about it. Your own shroombabies will grow when Turr is ready to bless them with the unique life. And when that day comes, you'll be a wonderful Dama to them."

Tears sparkled in Invidia's eyes as they nodded, warmth spreading through their body and spirit. "Thank you, Resley."

His bright smile lit up the world. "Now! About those vines you want to fight the humans with."

Invidia opened their bag, unable to refrain from dancing with anticipation. These new vines could bring an end to the corrupted croplands. They could bring Invidia a new beginning, a new purpose, a new way of caring for Turr.

With a gentle touch, Resley pulled five small vines from a patch of soft, cultivated soil. Their roots dragged along clumps of dirt that fell to the ground, scattering back into moist compost.

"I'll bring more compost next week, if you'd like." A pang of guilt and self awareness twisted inside them. "If I can remember," they quickly added.

Resley turned, a broad smile on his face, his blue eyes sparkling brightly. "You said that two weeks ago, and I'm still waiting."

Invidia's face burned red, but Resley only laughed.

"Don't think anything of it, Invidia. I know you'd rather spend your time running around the garden city than stomping in decay.

He wasn't wrong, but Invidia wanted to do better. Desperately, they wanted to conform, to file into their place in life, to serve Turr how every shroomperson was expected to.

Why did it seem such an impossible task?

Before they could promise to make it up to him, the planet beneath them groaned.

"What's—" Resley frowned, the words cut from his lips as a violent quake threw them to the ground .

The entire planet shook so violently, Invidia felt their flesh grind against the rocks below, the force rendering them helpless.

Resley yelled something, but Invidia's head throbbed too much to hear. When they touched their headcap, their hand came back covered in smashed, rubbery flesh. The world spun around them.

Warm hands hauled them to their feet.

"Run!" Resley dropped the baby vines, accidentally trampling them as he grabbed Invidia's shoulders. "Don't look, *run!*"

Invidia blinked, trying to straighten the world that only continued to spin in a blurry mess. Their head pounded, their body screaming in protest against the shaking ground, against the cuts lining their form. Screams filled the air. Sirens blared.

"Invidia! Just *go!*"

But they couldn't. Their eyes found the human city and the sight they beheld rooted them to the spot.

Huge fungi burst out of metal buildings. Vines

snaked up the alien structures, tearing them apart, prying the sheets of metal from their frames. Humans were thrown from the buildings, their screams chasing them before the sickening crunch of their bodies filled the air.

Turr was fighting back.

Their mind couldn't comprehend the horror. "What's happening?" They'd never felt fear before, not like this. Not in the way that they thought it would kill them if they felt any more of it. "What's going on?"

The roar of hundreds of jet engines filled their air. Alarms from the human city wailed. The smell of death wafted up to Invidia's button nose.

Resley spoke desperately, pushing against them, trying to herd them away to safety.

But Invidia didn't want to run away. They didn't want to be safe. They wanted to fight. To mean something.

With wide eyes, they stepped toward the chaos.

Explosions rippled across the land as the humans' shuttles lifted from platforms they hadn't moved from in years. Several crept into the sky, hanging still as if an invisible force held them back. Moments later, a few of the engines gave out. The ships fell to Turr's surface. Explosions and fire blinded Invidia, but even still, they didn't turn away.

The destruction was simply too overwhelming, the amount of death too incomprehensible.

Even Resley stopped fighting against them, frozen in place. Together, they watched the other shuttles take to the air, several of them exploding mid-flight. The sky rained with fire and metal. In the near distance, Isagani became pockmarked from falling debris.

"This isn't happening. This isn't real," Invidia whispered, but it was.

All of it was real.

Then, as if in one last attack against the planet they hadn't been able to tame or subdue, the humans pushed their ships into hyperdrive, dumping thousands of gallons of toxins into the sky.

For a long moment, everything fell silent as a haze of black death floated down toward Turr.

Then the sound of the planet's screams filled the air.

The planet shook, as if striving to flee the destruction.

The black haze settled.

The darkness began to spread.

Tight vines wrapped themselves around Invidia, sheltering them from the nightmare.

"It's going to be alright, Invidia." Resley whispered. tenderly. "Don't cry. Don't cry."

Invidia hadn't even known they were crying until they felt their wet face pressed against Resley's chest, his body quivering with the same fear that paralyzed their own.

"It's alright," he murmured as darkness filled the land. The moss beneath their feet began to turn black. Poison crept into their toes.

"I'm scared." Invidia wrapped their arms around Resley's neck, trying to ignore the darkness seeping through the veins of the vines growing from his body, encasing them in leafy protection.

But his protection wasn't enough.

None of their efforts had been enough to protect themselves against the humans.

Tears filled Resley's eyes as the void raced up his neck, darkening the blue in his gaze. "Don't be." He tried to smile, a single leaf brushing Invidia's shallow cheek. "Turr will take care of you."

Then the darkness consumed them too.

CLYRA

Day 2 Since the Humans Left

Night settled into its bones, an icy chill falling over the lab. The tracker in Yori's arm started flashing. The sudden light peeled back the dark, so cold and invasive that I had to avert my eyes.

It was the second night we'd been woken like this. I couldn't get used to the way the tracker grotesquely illuminated Yori's flesh from the inside out, the outlines of their veins traced across their pale skin.

They woke in a panic, lurching up and scrambling to wrap their arm in their blanket, but it was too late. The others had already begun to stir, the blinking light interrupting their sleep cycles.

"I'm sorry," Yori murmured, their eyes drooping with exhaustion. Their shroom headcap flushed with frustration and embarrassment. In the eerie light, I saw the way they balled their fists with each flash.

The room accepted their apology in silence. The flashing would stop soon enough, and darkness would regain its hold. Until then, we opened our eyes and reassured ourselves this new world still existed around us. We'd woken in captivity so many times, it didn't feel real for the world to be at our fingertips.

Yesterday, we pulled six beds into this room. Now that the doors were open, we didn't want to sleep alone anymore. as long as we gathered together. We'd be leaving at some point. We were just holding on for the moment, trying to build up the courage to take the next step.

I slipped out from beneath my blankets and made my way to Yori's side. They tucked themself around their arm to shield the room from the light. I brushed a finger against their skin and felt the electrical pulse that vibrated with each flash. It was bad enough the light woke us up, but them trying to hide their pain was a whole other burden.

"I'm so sorry, Yori." I pulled them close. The edges of our caps brushed, our skin sticky and warm in the cool night. I found peace in the light contact.

Yori held onto me tightly with one arm. "It's not your fault."

"I should've done more." I placed my hand over their arm.

Yori didn't respond. The humans implanted the tracker after their attempted escape. Though they'd escaped the humans' reach, the lab was only so big, and they could only do so much on their own. We'd failed them, all of us who'd watched without joining in. And when the humans had forced Yori to the ground to inject the large tracker into their arm, we hadn't made a sound.

Fear made us complicit.

I looked over Yori's shoulder at the others turning in their beds, struggling to fall back asleep. One bed in the room lay still. I pulled back from Yori, fear digging into my chest.

"What's wrong?" they asked.

"Can you give me some light?" I stood up, craning my neck to see everyone. Yori pulled the blanket off their arm, and the room lit up again. The others groaned feebly as they buried their eyes under arms or tattered covers. I walked across the room, names passing through my lips as I caught glimpses of faces in the blinding light.

"Straiya isn't here." I turned desperately, wondering if somehow I'd missed her in the lengthening shadows. I hadn't. Taking a deep breath, I grabbed onto the light building in my core. Glowing was a result of my species, not a curse like it was for Yori. The light started in my cheeks, running down my throat and spreading through the rest of my body. Gentle warmth followed the light. The blue hue brought comfort against Yori's blinding light.

The room filled with motion. Blankets rustled, quickly abandoned. Bare feet slapped on the stone floor. Only six of us remained in the lab. We couldn't lose another.

"Who spoke to her last?" Yori asked

"She was here. I saw her before I fell asleep." Leyren spoke from the back of the room. They sat on their bed, their back against the wall. We ignored the tear streaks running down their cheeks. We all dealt with our pain in different ways. Sometimes that pain didn't show itself until no one else was watching.

"She wouldn't leave the lab without us," Yori insisted. Though others in the lab had left when it happened, taking off into the wild as soon as the walls collapsed, their souls craving freedom, none of us were brave enough to leave on our own. Everyone in this room held back, unsure and scared. We'd become protective of each other, no bond greater than pain.

All at once, Yori's light went out, leaving us in the cold dark. I chased it away by brightening my own glow.

"She probably went out to clear her head," Leyren spoke up from behind me.

"One of you go and find her so the rest of us can sleep," Ighta snapped from their bed. "Now that Yori's not lighting up the room, I'd like some peace and quiet."

I stopped myself from snapping back. I couldn't see much of Ighta, their body wrapped in a cocoon of blankets, the back of their head facing me. The blankets stain black from the liquid seeping from their skin. They were the only one found to be poisonous to humans, making them a target in the twisted experiments. The scientists hunted for an antidote to Ighta's natural repellant, using all sorts of sharp tools to dissect them. Their skin still hadn't healed, a constellation of weeping wounds scattered across their worn body.

Yori hung their head uncomfortably, their eyes growing small. They looked over in Ighta's direction, mouth open and ready to bite back.

"Can we please not fight?" I asked softly. Between my sympathy for Ighta and Yori and my fear for Straiya, I was stretched thin. We'd all grown harsher during the human occupation of Turr. We'd lost connection with who we were meant to be. I didn't even feel like my body belonged to me anymore. It was just a shell that caused me pain.

I couldn't imagine how Ighta felt, their body falling apart more every day. And Straiya had lost the ability of flight because of the humans.

"Straiya can take care of herself. I'm sure she's fine." Leyren said. I turned and met their tired gaze. They slept without blankets, their tall form stretched across the small bed. In the dim light, their white skin glowed. Small mushrooms grew along their shoulders and down their back.

A hush bloomed across the room. Their worry for Straiya had quickly melted into the need for more sleep.

Rhyse watched me from the place where he slept. He shifted, his exoskeleton reflecting pieces of my light. "Let's go find her," he said, standing up. "She can't have gone far."

"Thank you," I whispered. I didn't want to face

the world on my own.

We paused at the door, fearful of our vulnerability to the destruction beyond. The mess Turr made when she imploded was catastrophically beautiful. On that day, while waiting for the next round of torture, the floor had suddenly erupted and Turr's arms had come to hold us, thick roots snaking through the tiles. Alarms rang, lights flashed, but not even human technology was a match for the fury of a planet.

In the aftermath, as the world shook and burned, blackened beneath the human exodus, we stayed lost in our sudden freedom. The lab, now more familiar than Turr, had become a home—dark and twisted as it was—and those of us who'd stayed became a family.

We waited for something to force us from the lab. We'd all heard the planet speak, telling us to find each other in order to heal. But we were already together. What more did we have to do?

We stepped out into the hungry world. I took the lead at first, a false sense of confidence flooding through me. My light glimmered hopefully. Rhyse followed right behind me. His breathing echoed loudly in the quiet dark, and I took comfort in the raw sound. It reminded me that I wasn't alone—a comforting and frightening thought.

I cast a glance behind me as Rhyse moved along, hardly visible in the darkness, his shell blending with the shades of night. He reached forward and took my hand. Contrary to the back of his hand—a hard exoskeleton plate—his palm felt warm. I pulled him beside me. The walls stretched out on both sides of us, but I didn't feel safe between them.

"Where do you want to look for Straiya?" he asked.

Straiya had recently taken to climbing things. She couldn't fly, but she could jump much higher than the rest of us. She'd told me that when she was on the ground, she could feel its weight pulling at her feet. I couldn't blame her for wanting to get away from it. I could only think of one place capable of taking her from the ground.

"We should check the roof," I said.

At the end of this hall stretched the lab's entrance. It opened up into a large room with various hallways and stairs leading to different sections of the small lab. Turr had struck there the hardest. Moonlight bled through gaping holes in the ceiling. Humans who'd fallen victim to Turr's wrath lay scattered across the ground. We avoided them, their bodies beginning to reek.

We reached the first flight of badly mangled stairs. Metal support rods desperately tried to hold the concrete together. They shifted under our feet, the lab creaking, shrieking, almost crumbling around us.

I expected to feel rough human hands urging me forward, to hear their strange words as they yelled at each other. Instead, I got Rhyse's reassurance as he started up the stairs.

We were taking back our planet one step at a

time.

The second floor ran around the foyer. A thin railing stood between us and the drop—an unsettling memorial to where Yori had thrown themself over in an attempt to escape. A chill ran through my pores. Their desperate screams as the tracker pushed deep into their flesh echoed in my memories.

"Are you okay?" Rhyse stopped.

"I don't like being up here." I observed the doors lining the hall. They hung open, the electronic locks useless, but I could still hear them slamming closed, sealing me into a small sterile room with the humans and their painful tests.

"None of us do. Just remember, everyone who hurt us is either dead or off the planet." He held me close, chasing away the dark with his presence. "They can never hurt us again. Turr made sure of that."

They didn't *need* to hurt us again. We still carried our wounds in their absence.

"Come," he beckoned, "look."

A large part of the wall had collapsed. We stepped toward the edge and listened to the wind as it spoke to the plants. I wrapped my arms around myself. The wind scraped against my soft skin.

Standing face to face with Turr, it seemed impossible to ignore her call to leave the lab. I hadn't touched her skin since the humans captured me. I'd changed since then, became a creature Turr might not even recognize. Had I let my scars define me? Had I let them change who I was?

I didn't know, and that unknowing filled me with incomprehensible fear.

The hardest part about dealing with human destruction was knowing it meant nothing in the end. They'd scarred Turr's beautiful skin, twisted her inhabitants into something unrecognizable, and left a legacy of senseless violence to live on without them.

We turned from the opening and looked for a way to the roof. An empty hole gaped where the next set of stairs had once stood, the rubble laying in pieces on the ground below.

"You think she got up there on her own?" Rhyse asked.

"I do." I scanned the space between us and the door. "Can you get me up to that?" I asked, pointing at the ledge at the top.

Rhyse frowned. "It doesn't look very safe."

"Maybe I'll fall and Straiya will find us when I scream." I laughed, trying to lighten the mood.

His face didn't crack. "I don't want you to get hurt," he said carefully.

"Just hold tight and don't let me fall. I'll be fine."

He let go of my hand and held his fingers together, making a step. I placed my foot into his palms, and he boosted me forward. I reached out and grabbed the ledge, which wasn't as wide as I'd thought. My fingers kept slipping, throwing my weight back onto Rhyse. He grunted, his arms shaking with effort.

I launched myself forward, ignoring his startled yell, and grabbed onto the sides of the door with my arms. I hung in terrified limbo, swaying, my legs kicking frantically. Rhyse tried to grab my legs. My hands searched for anything to hold onto.

I found a dip in the stone, wrapped my fingers around it, and pulled. My body burned with effort. The sharp edges of the stone dug into me, and my skin screamed. Before the capture, I could've done this easily. My time in the lab had weakened me. If I was going to survive in this rough version of the world I once knew, I'd have to build that strength back.

I got my knee onto the ledge, using it as a leverage to pull myself up the rest of the way. I lay on my stomach and sucked in the cold air. After a couple minutes of heaving, I pushed myself up and took in the view.

What a view it was. Turr had strangled herself in her desperate effort to get rid of the humans. Roots spread across the ground, leaving deep gouges in the soil. The fungus trees around the lab grew tilted. After Turr had pushed the roots up, the soil settled wrong.

Straiya stood on the edge of the roof. She didn't hear me coming up. I looked down at Rhyse's worried face and nodded, letting him know I found her. He sat down to wait for my return.

Straiya didn't move as I approached. She held her hands up, face pointing at the sky. Instead of a mushroom cap, a jelly skirt framed her face. Glowing strands grew at its center and hung down in braided threads, reaching to her waist.

I knew why Straiya had chosen to come out tonight. She needed to be *seen*, and what better place to be seen than beneath the eyes of the universe? The stars shone so brightly. Between them, other planets added bursts of light. The arms of the galaxy stretched from one horizon to the next.

"Straiya?" I reached out and gently grabbed her shoulder.

She spun, surprised, and her arm grabbed mine. For a moment there, I worried she'd fall back and pull us both off the roof, but she stabilized herself just in time. The light from my skin reflected off the tears streaming down her cheeks.

"Oh, Straiya." I wrapped my arms around her, and she collapsed against me. She cried until she couldn't anymore, then shook with the remaining grief. I held her tight until she pulled away. Her eyes moved back to Turr, and she sniffled.

"Everything is so broken." She spoke so softly I could barely hear her over the wind.

"I know." The words caught in my throat. I'd been hiding from this reality, staying inside the lab so I didn't have to take in the brokenness.

"How are we meant to fix this? How will Turr ever be *whole* again?"

The first of my own tears trickled over. An overwhelming amount of helplessness filled the crevices between our skin. We weren't capable of fixing this world.

Find each other and you will find me.

The words came to my mind again. They'd been spoken by Turr to every living being on the planet—a call to action. To war, even, against our drowning doubt.

Then in healing yourselves, you will heal me.

"Turr won't give up on us. She won't be broken for long," I promised, still holding Straiya in my arms. I believed Turr could recover from this. I believed she would be able to heal us all. When I saw the pain etched on our skin, I had to believe Turr could fix it.

If I didn't, what would be the point of living?

We'd been surviving, not living, and surviving *hurt so much.*

Taking all the turmoil inside, we released it in the only way we knew how. Crying at the edge of the roof was part of healing. Crying opened a cavity within us for healing to take root.

"How did you get up here?"

I laughed. "I was worried about you. I had Rhyse boost me up so I could see if you were here."

She laughed. "Thank you for noticing I was gone. I needed company, I just didn't know how to ask for it."

I squeezed her tightly. "We all need each other. Don't be afraid to ask for what you need."

She leaned against me a little harder, her weight almost pulling me down. "I think right now I need more sleep. Do you think we could sleep up here?"

I shivered. "It's too cold. Plus, it looks like it's about to storm." Dark clouds built along the horizon, slowly wiping away the stars. A brisk wind cut through the trees, bringing with it a horrible chill.

Straiya grabbed my hand, and we ran to the door, the smell of rain following closely behind.

INVIDIA

Day 3 Since Humans Made the Dead Zones

"Wake up," the wind whispered with the strength of a dying breath.

Invidia shivered, mind dysfunctional against the roaring pain coursing through their body.

Everything felt wrong. Where folds of their healthy flesh had once rested, the cold bite of the sharp air brushed instead, cutting deep into places that should never taste the sky. Their headcap rested uneven on the ground, unbalanced, like too large a piece was missing.

Wanting to scream, but feeling no strength to comprehend or process their own pain, Invidia pinched their eyes closed, willing the darkness to take them once again.

But the wind spoke persistently. "Wake up. Wake up. Wake up," it hissed over and over and over until Invidia forced their eyes open. The feeling of sand scraped across their lids as they blinked, beholding the world around them, facing nothing but more darkness.

A strangled gasp left their lips.

Silence rang in their ears, louder than any roar of the human's engines or rage in Turr's storms. They'd never known true silence until now, and they never wanted to know it again. But now, escaping seemed impossible. The deafening silence slipped under their pores, into their eyes, between their fingers and toes, drawing aching pathways where it trailed.

Pushing themself, they sat upright.

An unbridled scream escaped their peeling lips.

Destruction stretched for miles.

"No." They shook themself and dug their fingers into their arms, feeling slime where solid flesh had once sat. "No!"

The blackness wavered under a shimmer of green.

Thick, gritty tears streaked down their cheeks. Little strips of their skin peeled with the liquid, trickling down their neck, tickling them, making them reach for their own throat, wishing to tear it out.

"No."

The blackness wavered again.

Closing their eyes, they buried themself below the incomprehensible reality around them. They buried themself deep inside their own being, searching desperately for the now tainted memories of a Turr once green and full of life.

The aching slivers of their once vibrant psychedelic properties pulsed weakly through their mangled form.

"Nothing is wrong." They begged themself to believe their words.

The pain lessened. The air grew a little cleaner, the sky a little brighter.

"None of this is real," they whispered to themself, doing what they did best.

Lie.

After what felt like only a second and an entire lifetime, they forced their eyes open again, forced themself to believe everything they'd seen, all the death, all the rot, all the destruction, was nothing but a dream.

Stretching, Invidia looked around, trying to gain a hold of their surroundings. The air seemed hazy, foggy. The colors felt muted, like the filter of dawn had been placed upon the land, though, really, it looked mid-day. A flicker of fear stirred inside them as they gazed upon their hands. They seemed paler than usual, but when flecks of rot appeared, Invidia dragged their fingers across the spots until they disappeared.

Pushing on the ground to stand, they vaguely noticed the ground felt harder than they remembered. But the thought brought discomfort, and discomfort was quickly buried with every other unwanted memory and feeling, crushed until it couldn't raise its ugly head.

But they couldn't bury the silence—the aching, horrific, dense, permeating silence. No lie could hide that from Invidia. They wanted to scream just to fill the void, but when they opened their lips, breath burned their cells.

Where is the sound? Where is the chirp of the grasshopper? The flutter of the butterfly's wings?

A thousand excuses raced through their mind, but none that brought peace or comfort.

Invidia planted their hands on their slimy hips. Their grip slipped on rotting matter, once, twice, thrice. The sensation made their soul squirm. Tears burned their eyes as they refused to look upon their own body.

"It's just a bit of dew," they whimpered, speaking to no one but themself, filling the silence as best they could with the sound of their own raspy voice.

"Now . . . what was I doing here?" They raked their mind, trying to piece together how they'd arrived here. The harder they tried to think, the more their head throbbed. They remembered waking up one morning in a ring of diligently grown shrooms, but why weren't they at the compost pile with the other shroompeople?

Touching the back of their headcap, they felt the curve and dent where a piece of them was missing. "I think . . ." They frowned, biting back a wave of emotion that rose as a scream in the back of their throat. "I think I fell and hit my head. I need to get home. I need—" They cut themself off. They didn't want to *need* anything.

But something was wrong. Something was so horribly wrong. The landscape wavered between green and black around them. Agony coursed through their body in places they hadn't known existed before.

Pulled by force of habit, Invidia turned to where they expected to see Isagani rising in the distance. A thick fog covered the horizon.

Invidia picked at their bottom lip, the flesh chipping away easier than it should have. "Wait. It wasn't so foggy this morning." They squinted, yearning to see their home. The gray fog remained unyielding.

A tidal wave of dread coiled inside them—a feeling they most certainly didn't want to feel. Instead, they turned back to their immediate surroundings, promising themself Isagani stood tall behind the fog, awaiting their return.

"Well"—they brushed black dirt from their legs, picking off little heart-shaped vines that had twined there—"Resley should be around here somewhere. He'll know why I'm here, and why my head hurts so much."

A step forward elicited a loud *crunch*. They looked down, frowning at the dried woven lily-root bag under their feet. The foreign black plant matter, so foreign in stark contrast to the green grass it lay on, pulsed with familiarity. They reached to pick it up, and when their fingers touched it, green life rippled up and down its length.

"Oh!" Recognition flooded them with relief. "It's my bag! I was here, with Resley, gathering new seedlings to plant next to the humans' crops."

They didn't spend a moment questioning why the bag looked dead and dry before they touched it. Right now, it appeared as it should, and that was good enough.

"Now, where is Resley? He was just here." A small voice inside them said they were silly for speaking to themself with no one around to hear, but the silence in the air suffocated them if they didn't suck in breath to fill the void with words.

The road they started down stretched too hard, too rocky under their feet, but each time they looked down, confused, they saw nothing but soft moss. "What is wrong with this moss?" With a hesitant touch, they brushed their fingers across the moss, the growth scraping their flesh like sharp gravel. "By Turr. I need to let someone know this moss isn't healthy. I'm surprised Resley hasn't reported it already." Looking around, they expected to see other Turrians milling about the vine gardens.

Not even the wind moved.

Resolving that they'd send help for the moss as soon as they returned home, Invidia straightened and nodded definitively before skipping back down the path. They found it almost impossible to ignore the painful way the road dug into the soles of their feet. Almost.

One moment they skipped along with nothing but empty road in sight. Next, they collided against something, sending them sprawling to the unyielding, gravely path.

Tears filled their eyes as their bottom lip quivered. For a long moment, they simply held their scraped hands to their torn knees, willing the pain to go away. It refused.

With shaking fingers, they pressed against a lump in their thigh where they'd landed. A small rock sat lodged under the surface of their flesh, throbbing, screaming, aching. Swallowing the horror clawing its way up their throat, they dug their fingers into the hole where the rock entered.

Cold rot greased their fingers. Spots dotted their vision.

"Help me," Invidia rasped. "Please. Someone." Their body shook uncontrollably. No one answered.

With fingers that hardly responded, they poked and pried through their flesh until they felt the rock. Breathing deep, they pulled back hard. The rock tore through their leg, ignoring its path in and instead making a new path out.

A scream ripped from Invidia's lips, echoing across the valley, shattering the oppressive silence for just a second.

Shivering against shock, Invidia rocked back and forth, unable to tear their hand from the oozing wound, unable to look at the black pus seeping from their leg. They wanted to lay down, to ignore the impenetrable fog hiding their home from them, to forget the screams ringing in their mind every time they stopped talking, stopped filling the silence.

But they couldn't. They had to find Resley, make amends with Lorna, and fight back against the humans. They had to make a difference.

"And I can't do that if I break down here. Someday I'll grieve. Someday I'll understand this pain inside me. But not now. Not yet."

The pain faded to a dull ache. The colors around them grew a shade more vibrant.

Brushing off bits of crispy black moss clinging to their legs and torso, Invidia stood, staggering around to see what they'd tripped over.

A large rock covered in moss and little mushrooms stood unmoving in the center of the path. Frowning, Invidia limped back to it, running their hands over it. It didn't feel like a rock. Instead, it stretched smooth and cold under their touch, as if polished.

"That's not right. How did I not see this?" They could've sworn it hadn't been there moments before they'd tripped on it. "What are you?"

At that moment, the moss disappeared. Silver, cold, polished metal under a thin layer of soot reflected back a hazy version of themself. A wave of light-headedness washed over them. Raising their fingers, they watched as the reflection did the same.

"It's just the soot," they whimpered, turning their head side to side, unable to see their bright pink headcap or the rosy blush that once decorated their form.

Instead, a thin figure with black and pale ribbon-cut flesh stared back. Eyes looked on, hollow, haunted, soulless. But it wasn't them. It *couldn't* be them.

They weren't a monster.

The moss beneath them flickered before patches of it disappeared, exposing the rubble of burned earth and wreckage.

An explosion shook the planet. Screams filled the air. Metal jets blasted off Turr's surface, soaring unnaturally high as they attempted to escape the plants tearing through metal buildings, shattering glass, killing every human they touched.

Then the planet shook. Rocks cracked. Forests fell. Turr quivered and screamed as a black mist descended upon the planet.

Death rushed forth, unleashed, unbridled, hungry.

The vision disappeared. Invidia curled in on themself, balled up next to the moss covered rock. Gravel dug into their shoulders. Tears poured down their face. Sickness churned inside them. Rolling over, they threw up black sludge; it faded into the moss, disappearing almost as soon as it touched the ground. When they wiped their lips, the blackness on their pale skin faded away as well, though they could still feel its cold, heavy presence.

Stumbling to their feet and clutching their bag—the only thing that felt remotely familiar in this waking nightmare—they started running down the path. It wasn't until the vine forest grew up around them again that they realized they'd only run back to where they'd first awoken.

"No, no, no." They clutched their shrunken shroomcap, vaguely aware of how much smaller it was now. "No, I was just here. Why am I running *from* Isagani? I have to get back. I have to go home." Something called them to the gardens; something there needed their help. Invidia knew they had to go back, but the thought filled them with paralyzing fear.

"It's just a dream, just a hallucination. I'm a psychedelic shroom. This is normal." They repeated the mantra over and over as if repetition would create belief in it. But what was the dream? The green life around them that wavered and faltered or the memories of death too horrible and existential to be real?

"It's okay. I'm okay," they lied quietly. "I just need to get back home. It'll all make sense when I'm back in the gardens."

With a weak grip, they used a tall vine tree to pull themself to their feet. It snapped under their weight, sending them tumbling back to the ground with a grunt. A shiver ran down their back as panic raced up it. Closing their small fingers around the branch they'd broken, Invidia watched it crumble to powder before floating to the ground, disappearing.

"I have to get out of here." Scrambling to their feet and refusing to touch any other plants, they stumbled back down the path.

Against their better judgment, Invidia's eyes wandered to the side of the road. They wished they'd never looked.

A body lay partially hidden in the brush.

Their legs moving without consent, they tiptoed toward it, dread sinking in their chest. A name left their lips on its own accord. "Resley?"

Invidia crouched, slowly turned the green, leafy body onto its back, and screamed.

The entire front of the creature was charred. Tar-like decay had turned his eyes into dark orbs. Black rot dripped from where his lips used to be and from a wound on his chest where a piece of metal seemed to grow from his flesh.

Invidia fell back, muffling their screams in their hands. Fear and horror rooted them to the spot.

A memory tore itself free from their hallucination.

Resley wrapped a growth of heart-shaped vines around Invidia, cradling them close.

"Don't be afraid. It's going to be okay," he whispered just before the sky exploded with fire and toxins. Metal rained down around them, on them, into them—

"No!" Invidia pressed their hands over their ears, screaming against the memories, burying them deep within their mind once again. "No, it's not real!" The noise around them faded. The vision disappeared.

When they looked back at Resley, he'd sat up, smiling. "What's wrong, Invidia?"

Relief washed over Invidia as they brushed away their tears, gasping for a steady breath that didn't feel like poison in their cells. "I just keep having these really bad nightmares. Maybe I need to detox from some of the hallucinogens in my body. I think it's beginning to affect the way I see the world."

Smiling, Resley reached out a hand. Invidia took it, helping him to his feet, ignoring how cold his skin felt, though his smile shone as warm as the sun. "I still have those vines if you want them."

"I do." Invidia could just see parts of the human city peeking through the fog. "I have work to do. The humans need to be brought down."

"Then let me help you." He wrapped his arm around them, leaning on them heavily.

"Are you well?" they asked, worried as they staggered under their friend's weight. A stale smell wafted off him as he rested his head on their shoulder and breathed out.

"Yes. I'm just a little tired is all."

They nodded. "That's alright. I can carry you." Holding his hand, they took the majority of his weight onto their shoulders and slowly started down the road, making sure to walk around the mossy rock this time.

As they started their slow journey, Invidia ignored how odd it was that Resley's eyes never once opened, nor did he continue to speak, though he usually hated to walk in silence. They also ignored the way his feet dragged across the road.

"You just rest," Invidia whispered to his quiet, lifeless form. "I'm going to get us home."

CLYRA

Day 3 Since the Humans Left

In the early hours, Turr opened her skies and unleashed her rage. The storm lasted well into the morning. Thick clouds coated the sky, blocking out light, and the lab stayed dark.

Straiya and Rhyse put out buckets to catch the rain. When the roots broke through the lab, they disrupted the pipe system, cutting off fresh water. What remained didn't seem drinkable.

The rain hammered against the roof, drowning out our thoughts. At times, it seemed the shrieking wind would tear the lab apart.

Would Turr give the wind that power if we weren't inside?

I wrapped myself in a coarse blanket and lay in the safety of my bed. The blanket wasn't much of a barrier between me and the cold world. I turned to face the dark wall and tried to reach out to Turr.

Once, I'd spoken to her daily, our connection unbreakable. Now, I couldn't open up to her. I'd forgotten what it was to speak to our planet. When I tried to reach out, the words stopped on my tongue, forever bouncing around the confines of my mind. I was too broken, too helpless, too scared.

My hands unconsciously made their way to my face, and I wrapped them around the back of my neck. The world rested heavily upon me. I massaged my skin, trying to relieve the pain of holding myself together.

The urge to put down roots was strong. Roots meant different things to different Turrians, but to the shroompeople, they become a way of bridging the gap between us and Turr. I had no way of putting down roots. Not here, where a thick layer of concrete separated me from the soil.

Strange pain tingled across the bottoms of my feet. I rolled onto my stomach and buried my face in my pillow, the loud world closing in around me.

How exhausting it was to be alive.

How easy it would be to give up.

Rhyse carried one of the buckets into the lab. "Look at this." Rhyse held the bucket out for us to see. Murky, oily liquid filled half of it. A thousand colors danced across the surface. The sickly smell stuck to the air.

"That's the rain?" I held a hand to my stomach. Nausea rolled through me. First the humans took our planet, then they took our rain.

Rhyse nodded. "Everything we gathered from the storm is tainted with toxins."

It was bound to happen. All the waste the humans dumped would eventually permeate the planet's water cycle. The toxins would inevitably spread to every part of Turr. I just hadn't expected it to be so visible.

"What will we do?" Straiya asked.

I turned away, panic setting in. We couldn't escape the reality we lived in. The lab continued to fall apart, the water was undrinkable . . . what were we supposed to do?

Is this why the storm felt so relentless? Was Turr trying to purge herself of this disease? I couldn't imagine how she felt, a lonely planet with poison trapped in her atmosphere.

"We should consider the possibility that there might not be drinking water anywhere on Turr," I said soberly. I hadn't thought about the planet being deadly, but if the rain ran black, it would soak into every crevice of the planet.

"Wouldn't the others have come back?" Straiya slouched, defeated.

Would they come back to die here, or would they choose to die in Turr's arms?

Leyren placed a hand on Straiya's shoulder, rubbing circles on her skin. "I'm sure the others are fine. The toxins are probably temporary." They shot a wary glance in my direction. I saw my hopelessness reflected in their eyes.

"We have to believe that it's going to be okay. Turr will get rid of the toxins," I said bravely. I pushed away all the negative thoughts fighting for space. I couldn't burden myself with everything. "We should set buckets on the roof. If we keep catching water during the storms, we can check and see if it gets clearer. It will give us a way to monitor Turr's healing."

Straiya lightened up. "I can do that."

I smiled. "Perfect. Thanks."

She hurried out of the room, Leyren following behind. The little tasks made life more manageable. They kept us distracted, while making us feel like we were doing our part to fix the planet.

Only Rhyse stood by me now. "That was a good idea." He grinned.

I ran anxious hands across my face, trying not to let out a frustrated huff. "Thanks."

"I can't help but notice that some of them come to you with their problems. They must trust you."

I slouched forward. I'd noticed it too, and I wasn't happy about it. "I don't know why they expect me to be able to fix things. I'm just as scared as the rest of them."

"You do a good job of hiding it. To me, you just seem concerned about our wellbeing. You're a natural leader."

I hated that. I didn't want to be a leader in any way. I never asked for them to look to me for help. I wanted to shed their ideas of me like a second skin, but unfortunately skin didn't always listen to its inhabitants.

"It's not fair for them to expect that of me," I said.

"You don't have to step up."

I snorted. "Yeah, right. You saw how they were last night. No one was going to look for Straiya. No one cared enough."

"It's not that they didn't care. They just trusted Straiya to take care of herself. She was fine."

"She wasn't fine. She just looked fine when we came back. She's hurting. We're all hurting." I wrapped my arms around myself. "It's even harder for me because I feel like I have to hold their hurt alongside mine."

Rhyse shook his head. "You're not responsible for their healing, Clyra. You're suffering just as much as we are. Don't let anyone make you feel otherwise."

I couldn't help but feel they thought I wasn't as damaged because my body hadn't changed as drastically. I didn't have gaping pores or mushrooms growing out of my shoulders. My skin had lost its color, but that wasn't painful.

Yet underneath it, I was just as lost as them. I'd just gotten better at hiding it. A storm raged beneath my skin, and I didn't know how to stop it. The pressure of holding myself together in order to hold everyone else together threatened to split me in half.

"Clyra." Rhyse stopped, his eyes reading my face. "If you ever need to talk about anything, you can talk to me. You know that, right?"

I didn't know what to say. Approaching footsteps saved me from answering. Leyren stepped into view. "There you are," they said, their eyes moving between me and Rhyse. "You need to come and see this." Their words dripped with apprehensive excitement.

I nodded numbly, unable to put into words how much I'd rather not be this person for them. Leyren led us through the lab, over stretched roots and broken floor. The angry sky greeted us through the collapsed ceiling of the foyer.

One shroomperson had been killed during the exodus. Rhyse had carried their body out into the forest for Turr to take care of. We were all too aware that any of us could've died in their place. Yet Turr had done her best to protect us. The humans lay haphazardly across the room, many of them stabbed by roots or trapped beneath pieces of rubble.

"On our way through the lab, we noticed that the bodies seem to be shifting. Turr is taking them back." Leyren grinned.

Straiya and Ighta waited for us by one of the bodies. He curled around a root that pierced his chest, his open eyes watched the sky listlessly. Where his feet touched the ground, fungi and lichen climbed. I crouched, fascinated at the way the plants buried themselves in his skin, which flaked at their touch, peeling back to reveal muscle and coagulated blood. The small roots and spreading fungi slowly tore him apart.

The rot ate at him, unnaturally fast. His body looked soft. His head hung back, small roots reaching up to tangle in his gray hair and pull him down. His neck had begun to sever. Mushrooms bloomed from his eyes, nose, and ears. The decay eagerly devoured him, Turr desperate to swallow these bodies. Turr had always been a kind, yet violent planet. We didn't fear her for the same reasons the humans learned to fear her. She took care of her own. Even when that meant death in exchange for life.

We walked around the room. Each body was in a different stage of decay, the ground working hard to take the human flesh into itself. There was no overhanging stench, just the wet, earthy smell of a planet breaking free.

Ighta picked up a small stick and probed one of the bodies. The stick went right through the skin, revealing shining ribs. Ighta stepped back, sick curiosity crossing their face, and muttered a meaningless apology under their breath. I looked at them, then at the small hole in the torso of the dead woman. The ribs shone so white in the dark, they almost glowed beneath the translucent skin.

A peculiar feeling crept through me. A sort of calling. Before I knew what I was doing, my hand touched the skin, sinking into the collapsing flesh. Bone and muscle squished between my fingers.

My roots began to strain, working their way from the bottoms of my feet. They crept along the concrete, eager to devour. I stumbled back, the splayed roots tripping me. Sickness washed over me.

"Clyra," Ighta whispered, eyes wide with sick fascination.

I fled, running back through the halls, past our room, to the bathroom and shower stalls. I couldn't stand the smell coming from the toilets. I dashed into the nearest shower stall and emptied my stomach all over the tiled walls and floor. The burning in my throat became too painful to bear. I spit and spit until I felt empty, yet more tried to come up. I retched, my body stretching. A string of bile dangled from my lips.

Bending over like this, my insides trying to come out, overwhelmed me. I fought the urge to collapse and not get up. My entire body hurt. My mind had started screaming somewhere during the run and wouldn't stop.

I couldn't escape the blood on my hands, couldn't escape the fissures of my mind. This was our new life. No matter what happened, we would carry these scars until we died.

I stumbled toward the sinks. The far wall to my left had fallen, bits of Turr creeping in. Small sprigs pushed their way through tiles. Once our home, Turr had become a battlefield. Her presence advanced with every piece of life. Thick roots braced against the ceiling, holding it up. I started to think that maybe the roots were the only thing keeping the lab standing.

Turr was waiting for us to leave.

A shattered mirror hung above the sink. The cracks spread from an impact near the top, a thick spider web of illusions. I locked eyes with the multiple versions of myself and wondered which one was accurate. In all of them stared back a pale, dying creature. My skin, drained of its natural red hue, now matched the sickly pink of the human captors.

I fought the urge to pick up a shard of glass and cut myself out of my skin. I just wanted to find a way out. Surely a layer inside me remained true to myself.

I twisted the tap and water bubbled out, a stream too weak to wash away the blood. It stained, sinking into my soft flesh. I scrubbed and scraped, and the water continued to run pink.

Then, all at once, the water gushed black. The faucet screamed with pressure. I stepped back to avoid the water splashing up across the edge of the sink. My foot twisted beneath me, throwing me sideways. Frantic, I grabbed onto a root **and the world shifted sideways.**

In the blink of an eye, darkness crept across the room, turning it to rot. Dust motes hovered in the air. A thick, sticky stench choked me. I tried to pull my fingers away from the root, but they remained stuck. The rivers of time ceased flowing around me.

A whimper crawled up my throat. No, something else. Something alive. I spit on the floor and a beetle crawled out of the saliva. I felt them now, my inner cavities full of the worst kind of

life—death-eaters. They crawled inside me, carving tunnels through my heaving flesh.

I hung in the middle of the room, rooted in place through my fingers, my insides itching from the swarming insects. I screamed as they covered my tongue and moved behind my eyes. They burrowed through my limbs. I'd never been so full of life, yet so close to death.

They emerged, violently evacuating my body. My skin tore as they leaked from my pores. Their wings opened, and they filled the air around me. They swarmed before flying through the opening in the wall, leaving behind a bloody, broken body.

I felt no pain. In some detached way, I knew this wasn't real. My brain strove to translate the images and try to match them to my senses. It couldn't fabricate the feeling of my body coming apart.

In the end, me and my torn skin stood against the twisted world. I'd been left fully exposed and vulnerable, prey waiting for its predator. I'd completely fallen off the knife of reality. Whatever nightmare this was drowned me.

The leaves near the lab rustled. Footsteps moved through the underbrush. I heard them coming closer, and I closed my eyes. I couldn't feel pain, but the fear was real. It flooded through me in an overwhelming deluge.

A dark figure emerged from the shoulder-high ferns. They stepped forward, the dim light of the lab washing over them. Their deformed shape stood so alien in the night. I tried to turn and run, but my feet couldn't find purchase on the smooth floor. I fell limp, hanging from the root, at the mercy of the beast outside.

I couldn't figure out their shape. I saw the curve of a mushroomcap, but another bulbous growth by their neck turned them into a monster. When they stepped into the lab, I distinguished the lines and realized it was a whole other body. It lay draped over their shoulders, limbs melting into the shoulders and torso.

Death itself clung to them.

They spoke, the two of them, a half-dead shroomperson conversing with a vacant shell. Even though their eyes locked on me, I knew the words weren't directed at me. Not meant for my ears, I couldn't make them out.

I surrendered to their approach. They crossed the tiles and looked over my broken body. Reaching out a hand, they cupped my chin, lifting my face until I met their eyes. I lost myself in them, so dark and full of pain. The very ache of existence glimmered within them.

"I've been waiting for you," they whispered.

I couldn't look away from the body hanging across them. They wrapped an arm around it, unwilling to let it go. The gentle longing in that horrific display broke me in two. This was the extent of the human touch. This was what their exodus looked like. I had to wonder, just for a moment, if it was worth it.

I wanted to hold them like I had Straiya, like they held the shell of death on their shoulders. I wanted to offer any sort of peace I could. I felt myself getting dragged from this space. Their hands slipped off my skin, and the world jolted, throwing me back into focus.

I fell to the cold ground. My body burned as I breathed deeply. Panic sparked throughout my body in the aftermath of the visceral vision. I scanned the room to make sure I was alone.

The ferns swayed, void of any shroomperson. I stayed on my hands and knees, heaving, trying not to let myself cry.

"Clyra?" Leyren knocked on the wall outside the bathroom door. "Can I come in?"

I lay on the dirty floor, feeling invasive in my own skin. I let out an uncommitted sound, and they cracked the door open, slipping in. They dropped beside me, their warm hands burning on my cold skin.

"Oh, Clyra." Leyren helped me stand. "Here, let's get you washed up."

Leyren guided me to the sink. I felt sticky saliva on my chin and shuddered. The water no longer gushed. It dripped periodically, the white sink stained black. We watched the thick liquid slowly bubble down the drain. The pipes leading to the bathroom were finally empty.

"Well, that's a shame," Leyren muttered. They

glanced at me. I felt disgusting beneath their kind eyes. "It doesn't matter. We're all a mess."

I laughed. We *were* all a mess, but I still didn't want to smell like blood and vomit. I appreciated the way Leyren tried to comfort me, strange as it was. They cracked a smile. Their hands still held onto me. If they hadn't been here, I think I would've fallen apart again.

"Don't worry about what happened back there. With the humans, I mean."

That strange hunger gnawed away at me. I'd recognized the energy within the body, and my roots had acted accordingly.

"I don't even want to think about it."

Leyren held my face tenderly. "You have nothing to be ashamed of. Before we came to the lab, we would break down all sorts of rotting things."

"Not . . . like that." My stomach rolled.

"Humans are an invasive species. They're like the thick weeds that used to choke out the daffodil trees. Surely you remember when they were spreading across Turr?"

Their words unlocked memories I forgot I had, memories of cutting down thick clumps of weeds and letting them rot in piles before breaking down their mushy remains and taking their energy for myself.

"It doesn't feel the same."

"Well, it should. We're tired and we need energy. Those of us that break down the dead should try to break down the humans. We need to get rid of them." Leyren gave me a hug, ignoring my smell and the mess splattered across my body.

"Don't touch me so much. I'm gross." I pushed them away.

"The rains will fall and the mess will wash away. Stop feeling like such a burden." They opened their arms again, inviting me back in.

I sank into their hug. It had been a while since I'd felt this sort of care. With my chin buried in their neck, it was impossible to not notice the mushrooms growing along their shoulders. I hadn't taken much time to understand their pain. I noticed the way the mushrooms on their skin moved independently. The skin bubbled around the growths, the marks alarmingly familiar. I thought of the beetles evacuating my body, thought of the skin splitting around their glossy bodies. Leyren didn't need a vision to experience that. It was written across their skin.

"Do those hurt?" I asked.

They looked down at the mushrooms, surprised

at my question. "They did at first, but the pain has become part of who I am." They twisted to show me the mushrooms continuing down their back. The mushrooms were a vivid red, dark veins gathering along the tips. The stark contrast against Leyren's pale skin, a sky of mottled stars, mesmerized me.

"How do you deal with all that? How do you keep living when you feel like you're dying?"

Their hands tightened around me. "I don't feel like I'm dying. Not anymore. If anything, this makes me feel more alive. I wake up each morning and I know I'm still here."

I tried not to cry, but the tears already dripped from my eyes. Leyren hushed me and cradled my face between their hands. They pressed their forehead to mine. "What's wrong?"

"I can't push through the suffering anymore. I need to feel cared for. I've been caring for everyone else and waiting for someone to care about me. I had a vision. It was the first time Turr spoke to me, but it wasn't about me. It was so dark. I just wanted her to have something to say to *me*."

It was so incredibly selfish to say it out loud, but the moment the words passed between my lips, I felt better. I'd spoken my feelings. What happened next was out of my control.

"I'm sorry you feel that way. We're all doing our best here. We're alive, and that's what matters. Everything else will fall into place."

"But what about the things we can't change?" I

thought of my fading skin and their abnormal mushrooms.

Leyren pointed at a rough patch running across the top of their right shoulder. "I tried to pull the mushrooms out when they first started growing. It left a mess behind and hurt even more. I haven't tried again. Perhaps we aren't meant to change back. Perhaps we're meant to carry scars from the humans' time here."

"So this is who you are," I stated. All this pain, all this brokenness.

They took my hand. "This is who we all are."

Broken and in pain, but ready to fight for what should be ours.

The rain came back in the afternoon, this time cleaner, the earlier storm having cleansed the sky. Straiya helped me to the roof, and we stood beneath the freezing water. It gathered in the buckets, and we drank handfuls of it, giddy in our connection to Turr. I scooped some up and used it to wash my skin. Being clean helped me feel whole.

Whoops rang up from below, and we watched as the others ran in the wild, throwing their heads back to catch the water in their mouths. The ground ran black with toxins as it splashed around their feet. We'd stopped fearing for our health. The humans stole everything from us. We deserved to revel dangerously in our freedom.

I retreated from the edge and lay down on the roof. With my eyes closed and the rain falling around me, I felt as though I'd joined the song of life. It washed things from inside me. Bad things. Worries and stress, the fear of Turr rejecting me, all of it purged from my system.

The lab trembled beneath us. A startled shout cut through the air. Straiya grabbed my arm and pulled me up as a small part of the lab collapsed.

Amid the hammering rain extended a stunned silence. Then Rhyse pumped his arm and cheered. I laughed, unspeakable joy flooding through me.

The lab would not stand as a permanent scar on Turr's body.

I followed Straiya and we looked at the ruins from a safe distance. The lab didn't feel as sturdy as it had before. Pieces of the ceiling stuck up into the sky, exposing all sorts of strange human machines to the world. Turr would grow over them and break them down.

"We're going to be okay," Straiya said, leaning against me. She'd spotted the anxiety in my eyes. "Turr takes care of us in life and in death."

I echoed the words. We were part of the cycle of existence. We would give what we could through life, then repeat it after death. Through it all, Turr would not abandon us.

"Do you feel ready to leave?" I asked.

She smiled, her skin glowing in the rain. "I don't know if we'll ever feel ready to leave, but the new world is calling us. It's time we answer."

INVIDIA

Day 3 Since Humans Made the Dead Zones

"Invidia? What're you looking at?" Resley smiled unsurely as Invidia pulled their gaze from the thick fog hiding Isagani and most of the human city.

Their mind rang and buzzed. "Oh, um, nothing . . . I just thought—" They shook their head, rubbing their fingers against their temple. Why did none of this feel . . . right?

After spending almost six years working in the dirt and compost of Isagani, they'd learned to listen to the ebbs and flows of Turr's mood. Usually, they could easily tell when she was happy with the life on her skin, or when she sensed something was wrong with the plants and let her creatures know of it. It started as a knot in their gut, then grew until their hands trembled and eyes darted side to side, looking for the anomaly.

"You just thought what?" Resley's eyes darkened, his voice wavering and distorted.

"Resley?"

His hand dropped to their shoulder, feeling a bit too heavy, a bit too hard, unlike how soft and gentle his vine hands usually were. "Yes?" he whispered.

Invidia's eyes locked back onto the human's city. "Are those . . . *mushrooms* growing out of the metal buildings?" The fog shifted, hiding their view again. But they knew what they'd seen.

Silence stretched between them with a growing dissonance.

"I have those vines you were wanting. Did you bring a wet bag?"

"Yes." Invidia waved at him dismissively. Hadn't he said that before? They shrugged his hand off their shoulder as he tried to turn them around. "But I don't need the vines if the human city is already being destroyed. Right?"

The air around the metal city shimmered and wavered, flickering like a heat illusion. Something like a violent storm swirled around it, shredding more and more of the remaining buildings—an ongoing fight not yet won.

"Invidia, did you hit your head? I don't think you're feeling well. What are you talking about? Look at me."

Finally, they turned to him. The knot tightened in their gut, reminding them something wasn't right.

"The human city. I thought I saw mushrooms growing out of it and a storm pulling it apart. That's not *right*, is it?" Had they taken their lie too far and hallucinated mushrooms on the city? Or were they really growing from unnatural heights where no nutrients could be found?

Resley's hands cupped their face, but instead of smelling like clean rainwater, he smelled only of rot and decay. Shaking their head, they tried to free themself from his hold, but his hands clamped down on their face. The pain returned to their head, to their hands, to their thigh, reminding them of the damage they'd sustained. Damage and pain that begged for them to succumb to the rot.

"You're not making any sense, Invidia." His voice sounded strained, harsh.

"No," they whispered as **his eyes grew dark, and black goop began to seep out of them, out of his ears, his nose, his mouth.**

"The humans have never been here. There was never a city, there was never an explosion. No one is dead."

But he was.

With a cough that sent a spray of black all over Invidia's face, Resley collapsed onto them.

Their scream broke off in their throat as they staggered under the stone-heavy weight of him. His body turned from green to black before sloughing off in big, rotting chunks.

As his body melted down theirs, collecting in a puddle at their feet, they looked down at their hands. The black toxins soaked into their skin, their flesh, feasted on fatty cells until their arms were no thicker than twigs, creeped up their arms

and into their torso, head and legs. The screams in their chest finally broke loose.

Stumbling and slipping over slick, rotting, putrid plants, Invidia took off running. They didn't care where they went. They only wanted to get away. Away from the explosions, away from the black death spreading across the land, away from their rotting, dead friend.

Something slammed into the ground next to them and they startled, falling over a black moss covered rock steaming and smoking with fire and death. When they pushed themself to their hands and knees, they found themself staring down into the half-gray, half-colorful face of an apis Turrian—a honeybee shepherd.

"Help me," the creature rasped, reaching a dark hand toward Invidia. Their wings buzzed slowly as the toxic death raced through them, darkening their iridescent shine. "Help me!" The decaying hand wrapped around Invidia's wrist with more strength than the shroomperson expected.

"Let me go." Poison from the bee creature pierced Invidia's already damaged flesh like a thousand knives. Panic gripped their heart. They didn't want to be stuck here with this creature, left to die. They wanted to help the apis Turrian, to save them, but they didn't want to die trying. In fact, they didn't want to die at all. "Let me go!" With one last pull, Invidia felt something give as they stumbled back, falling into the crispy black moss. A soft scream and groan filled the air as Invidia stumbled to their feet, looking down at their own arm. The honeybee's hand still gripped Invidia's wrist, having been torn from its body.

Flailing, Invidia screamed, smashing the hand against a nearby rock until it turned to dust. Then, ignoring all cries and pleas from the dying creature, they took off running into the forest again, as far away from the human city as they could.

Purple glittering waters beckoned them. Desperate to cleanse themself of the toxins, they didn't think twice about running into the stream.

Every step they took grew more and more strained. "No, no, no."

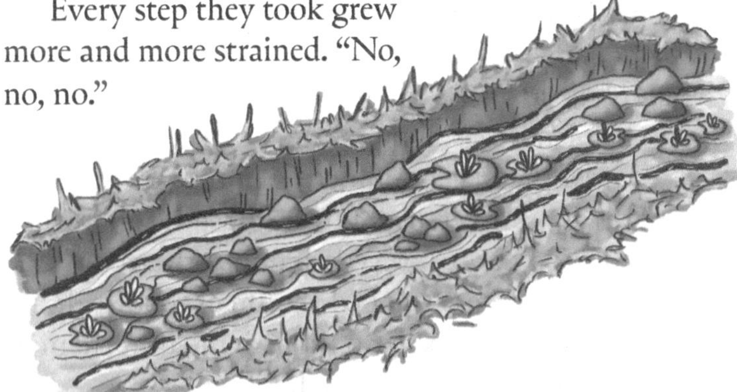

Whimpers escaped their lips as they helplessly tried to drag their feet from the tar-like goop overtaking the stream. The clear, purple waters were nowhere to be found, and the black poison wouldn't let go as easily as the bee's hand had.

"No, no. I don't want to die. I don't want everything to die!" Invidia let out a feral cry as they held their head, their little shroomcap shriveled and black, half the size it'd once been. "I don't want this to be real! I want to wake up!"

When they opened their eyes, some of the plants flickered from black to green, and the water below ran purple. Tears of relief dropped from their face to the waters, disappearing in their clear purple shimmer.

But when they tried to move, their feet remained stuck. Panic bound their chest.

"Turr! Don't leave me like this! Please, help me!"

No one answered

Covering their face, Invidia sank to the waters. Their vision of everything being alive and green faded. The world around them darkened until they couldn't lie to themself any longer.

The planet was dying.

Slowly, the black goop claimed their torso, then one arm. They stretched, fingers grasping air as they reached for a dark root twisting into the goop. The tips of their fingers gripped the small root. It didn't give way. A small flicker of hope ignited in them as the last of their strength faded.

"Help me," they whispered softly between sobs. "I don't want this to be the end."

For a long time, Invidia let themself space out into the darkness, unsure of how much time had passed. Their only grounding to reality was their grip on the little root.

Finally, a distant whisper drifted toward them.

"Hello?" Struggling against the goop, Invidia lifted their head and cried out with a raspy voice, "Hello! Please, anyone, help me!"

The wind blew so softly, Invidia almost believed it was another hallucination. Then it blew again, and this time, they thought they heard it whisper, **This is not the end. Let go . . .**

The air Invidia sucked in stabbed like a hundred knives. But every breath they took as the breeze kissed their cheeks felt like a promise. The moment passed as terror swallowed the comfort.

"Let go of what?" They bit their lip, wishing they could brush the tears from their cheek.

No one answered.

"Let go of what?" Invidia screamed, their grip on the root tightening. If they let go now, they'd be lost to the toxic sludge around them, if they weren't already.

Fear ached in their chest, opening a pit they didn't think would ever be full again. "I just want to live again. I want everything to make sense." Choking as the blackness pushed past their lips, seeped into their throat, their breath slowing, they whispered, "I just want to know my purpose again."

The wind sighed once more before everything fell silent. **Let go.**

But Invidia refused to give up. Not now. Not yet.

With a visceral scream, they pulled on the root, half expecting it to give way. When it didn't, and they felt the sludge give around their ankles, they cried. Tug after agonizing tug, Invidia stretched themself closer to the root.

The flesh in their shoulders stretched, threatening to tear. They strained, determined to pull their right arm free. Something in their shoulder tore before their arm finally slipped free of the muck.

Despite the burning pain in their body, they forced their other hand to grip the root and pull. With a sickening, sucking sound, their body emerged from the poisoned river.

Hand over hand over hand, they pulled until the last of the goop released them, and they fell onto the hard mossy bank.

Their arm hung limp and lifeless by their side, its unnatural angle crooked against their form, not quite how it should be.

Tears poured down their hollow cheeks, dropping onto the gravely death under their head, collecting into little blue and black droplets. For a moment, Invidia believed they saw the moss turn from black to green under their tears, as if the little water droplets were bringing life back to the planet.

But when they blinked, the moss turned black once more.

Squeezing their eyes shut against the darkness, against the truth, they tried to remember the way things had been before the humans' fall.

Green. Colorful. Beautiful.

It was a lie. Invidia knew the darkness that rotted beneath their touch. But one little psychedelic lie wouldn't hurt that much. At least, not as much as the truth did.

When they opened their eyes, hallucinated life covered death.

With quivering limbs, they pulled themself to their feet and forced their shoulder back into place as best they could, willing the hallucination to mask the tears in their rubbery flesh.

Step after step carried them through the grayish haze and manufactured life until they reached the road again. Until they saw their friend, motionless on the ground. They froze, wanting to leave him, to no longer have to gaze upon his still face and breathe his awful stench. But without him came the silence, and with the silence came the burning need to scream and scream and never stop screaming until all their pain merged with Turr's.

Reaching out, Invidia touched his cheek, ignoring how his flesh caved under their touch. "Wake up, Resley."

His eyes opened. "I'm awake. I never went to sleep."

Smiling unsurely, Invidia nodded. "I know. But it's time to move again. We have to get to Isagani, to the others."

He blinked, but didn't make any other movements. "Alright. Let's go."

Invidia chewed on their bottom lip, tasting dirt and rot. "Then get up."

Something like a lopsided grin stretched across his leafy green lips. "I—I can't today, Invidia. You'll have to carry me. I just don't . . . I don't feel good."

He's dead, some small voice whispered in Invidia's mind. *He didn't survive the blast. He didn't survive the toxins. He's not here anymore. Let Turr claim him.*

But they shook their head, angrily brushing away the tears running down their pockmarked cheeks. With a gasp, they wrapped his arm around them, shouldering his weight. They ignored how much heavier he felt today than yesterday. Ignored how their injured flesh sagged and stretched under the strain.

"Thank you, Invidia. Thank you for not leaving me."

"Of course. I'll never leave you behind."

But as they dragged their shaking legs down the road once again, the images of giant rainbow-colored fungus trees, shining glowing ferns, and little purple dew droplets shimmering and wavering as if breaking, a small part deep inside Invidia wondered if they should've left him behind.

If they should've **let go.**

CLYRA

Day 4 Since the Humans Left

I woke up with the sense that something had changed. I couldn't shake the feeling of being watched, though a quick look around the room confirmed everyone slept on.

The room felt fuller.

I lay still and waited for the feeling to pass. In the unbearable quiet, beneath the gentle sounds of breathing and blankets rustling, loomed something more ominous. The oozing, seeping sound of something slowly spreading filled the air, and above it lingered the smell of Turr.

I sat up and studied the dark room. A pit of dread planted itself in my stomach. I called on my light, the gentle blue warming the dark space. It reflected off faces, bounced off walls, but the far wall devoured the light, something black creeping up it.

Unable to hold myself back, I stood and made my way to the wall. The light revealed all manner of plants growing across the cold stone. I pressed my hand to it, sticky plant matter latching to my palm. Mushrooms grew at a visible rate. Large white stems ate away at the walls, their pulsing bodies digging into the concrete. Smaller fungi created a thick sap that coated the walls. Other plants crept next to them, continuing the invasion. A large bug buzzed past my ear, only for a carnivorous plant in the upper corner to lash out and snap it up. I almost shrieked. The crunch of the bug's shell echoed.

I watched the creeping life consume the wall. If Turr was going to give us a sign that we had to leave, this was it. She'd made it clear we were meant to be far from the lab by now.

I just didn't want to be the one to say it.

Already, I had filled some sort of leadership role in their minds. If I took charge of us leaving, I'd be forced into this role for the rest of my life. I couldn't lead the rebuilding of Turr. I couldn't even *step* onto Turr's surface.

The orange sap had completely covered my hand. In the dim light, it looked like blood. It felt warm against my skin, like holding a comforting hand. Life pulsed within it. The roots of growing plants stretched to their limits, working their way around my fingers.

They reached my wrist before a suffocating feeling swallowed me. I ripped my hand away, the porous sap dripping from my skin. I hated the way it echoed as it dripped.

Plink.

I ran from the room, holding my hand away from my body.

Plink.

I stood in the main entrance of the lab with a bucket of water. I'd planned to step out onto the soil before pouring the water, but standing here—facing Turr—left me paralyzed. I hadn't touched the surface of my planet in so long. I ached for it as much as I feared it.

I held the bucket out. The water swirled a worrying tone of gray. I tipped it forward, the cloudy water sloshing forward. We'd collected the water, washed ourselves with it, and enjoyed its taste. Who knew what coursed through our bodies now.

I poured the water over my hand and scrubbed. The sticky residue grew hard beneath the cold water, and I slowly worked it off my skin. Even in the growing light, the sap looked like blood. We were all bleeding in our own way. How much more could we bleed before we ran out of life?

As I washed, I found myself in the reflections of puddles below me. I locked eyes with the hollow shell staring up at me. As with the shattered mirror in the bathroom, this was a not-quite-right version of myself. I wavered in the ripples, my body stretching with the ebb and flow.

I had to leave this place. The more I thought about it, the more I was sure. I'd lost many of my memories from before the human invasion. The more they'd studied me, the more of myself I'd handed over to them. Maybe my memories were trapped in vials somewhere in the lab. Maybe when the lab collapsed, my memories would be released into Turr's skin.

I didn't yearn to hold onto my memories. The others clung to theirs like lifelines, and it changed them. They lived in the past instead of fighting for the future. I had to cut my memories loose in order to set myself free. Existing through the lens of what I lacked hurt more than the human's experiments.

I set the bucket down and shook my hands dry. The first hints of daylight entered the dark sky. The others would be up soon. They'd see the wall and come to the same conclu-sion I'd come to.

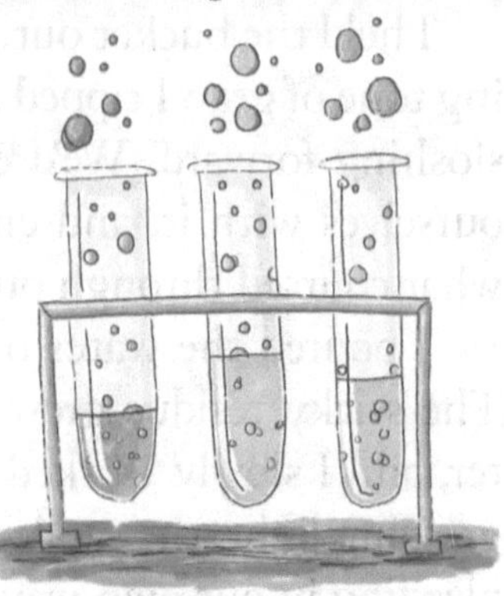

Was I ready to face them?

Perhaps if I could just touch Turr, I'd feel calmer.

I lifted my right foot and swung it out, testing the air above the dirt. All I had to do was take a step. One step. Turr would see that I trusted her to care for me.

My leg hovered for what felt like hours. The wind blew around me, the sound of the world beckoning, but my foot did not fall. I couldn't gather the courage to do this on my own. I stumbled back, guilt cutting through me, the pain of being a coward like a blade against my throat.

Where could I go from here?

Leyren sat in the center of the lobby. Human bodies lay around them, piled on top of each other in a messy circle. None of them were whole. Turr had been busy, her plants eating away at the flesh and bone.

"Leyren?" I stayed back, frightened. They didn't look up. I took a step closer, chills running through my body. "Leyren, can you hear me?"

Their eyes slowly rose to meet mine. I saw myself echoed in them, a body haunted by pain, loss, and a longing to be free of itself.

"Don't come any closer," they warned.

"What are you doing?" I took in the bodies, the way Leyren sat centered among them, the creeping white strands wrapping around breaking skin.

Roots.

Leyren was setting down roots among the dead.

"Don't look." They wilted beneath my gaze, their roots faltering among the bodies. "Don't look at this, Clyra."

I recognized the fear and the hunger fighting within them. They were desperate for the energy, desperate for healing, desperate to feel some connection to Turr.

"Oh, Leyren." The words exited so quietly, a

pained exhale as I realized just how afraid of me they were. "You don't have to hide this from me."

Yesterday, they'd assured me my hunger was natural. Now, driven by their desire, they were realizing just how hard it was to reconnect with the part of themself that drew comfort in devouring death.

I knelt on the outside of the ring. The gray bodies looked my way through vacant eye sockets. Turr watched me through the plant growth.

Tenderly, I touched one of the bodies. It fell apart beneath my fingers, too delicate to stand against the life straining against my skin. Energy hummed beneath the death.

It waited for us to claim it.

"Are you going to join me?" Leyren asked.

Join them, as if we were two friends sitting down to eat together and not two decaying beings at the end of the world.

I placed my hand on a bare patch of flesh and let the hollow hunger break free. I controlled it, then it controlled me. The roots appeared wherever my skin touched the ground, full of want, ready to be satisfied.

I was overwhelmed by the energy coursing back to me, the clear presence of Turr as she met me in my hunger. Hunger turned to rage, rage turned to violence. Roots twisted and tore through brittle bones and melting muscle. The bodies fell apart at our wish.

We held power here, where humans were dead and we remained.

We held power because even in death we would still remain, growing, coming back stronger, battling for this planet by Turr's side.

This war was never about us. It was about Turr. We were all a part of Turr. From her we came, to her we would return, cycling over and over through times of disaster and times of peace.

Through it all, Turr would prevail.

She would never be taken again. We would fight to the death and beyond to keep ourselves free, and free we would remain. Free in the knowing that we were eternal in ways these humans couldn't understand.

"Are you okay?" Leyren's voice broke through my heavy stream of thoughts.

I began shaking, crying, heaving, my roots too much and too little at the same time. Slowly, they retracted and I became a simple shroomperson trying to make it through another day.

"I will be okay," I said, my voice shaking. "We're heading home, Leyren. This will all be behind us and we'll never come back."

Home. What a foreign concept. Nothing but a memory. Yet it would soon be a reality, and I could not wait to experience it in its fullness.

I followed Leyren through the brightening lab. I felt more alive than ever, my insides split between delight and disgust. I'd been avoiding the humans, yet now I held them in me in a way I never dreamed possible.

"That was . . ." Leyren reached back and grabbed my hand. "It was incredible. For once, *we* held the power." They turned their head, their eyes catching mine. "Thank you for joining me."

I tipped my head down and hid beneath the edge of my cap. "What will the others think?"

Leyren stopped, and I stumbled into them. "You have to stop worrying about what they'll think." They grabbed my chin gently, angled my face up so I couldn't avoid their eyes. "What we did was healing for us, and that's all it has to be. It doesn't matter if it grosses them out. We didn't do it for them."

They waited for me to respond, but I had nothing to say. We resumed our walk in silence.

The others had awakened now. Their voices carried through the hall. Leyren's pace quickened, and I tried my best to keep up. We entered the room, everyone swiveling to look at us. Yori and Rhyse stood by the living wall.

"There you are," Straiya said. She sat up, a blanket wrapped around her.

Leyren pulled me up beside them. "You won't believe what me and Clyra just did." They gestured excitedly. "We feasted on some of the human bodies."

Yori gasped. "With your roots?"

I covered my mouth to hide my laugh. Leyren shot Yori a dark look. "No, we tore them apart with our hands and chewed them. Yes, with our roots."

Yori looked away, embarrassed. I placed a cautionary hand on Leyren's shoulder. I didn't want them to hurt the others.

"Was it weird?" Straiya leaned forward, curiosity glimmering in her eyes.

"It felt good," I responded. "It felt natural. I don't remember the last time I put down roots, but I need to start doing it more often."

Leyren nodded. "It was amazing. I finally feel ready to leave this place."

"We're leaving?" Ighta looked between us, their eyes narrowing. "So soon?"

"Come on, Ighta. You knew we'd be leaving. We should've left by now."

Ighta laughed. "Left while the rain was black and the winds blew like a knife? You think we would've survived that?"

"The others did."

"Did they? Or were they unable to come back? For all you know, we'll head out there and find their bodies." Ighta shook their head with disgust. "I don't think we should leave yet. We're not ready to see what Turr has become."

"We will be if we go back to who we're meant to be," Leyren argued stubbornly. "Think about it. We used to return the dead to the ground. At least I did, and Clyra and Yori and Ighta too. Rhyse should be out gathering food from the trees. He's meant to be climbing. Straiya—" Leyren's voice cut for a moment, almost as if they regretted what they were about to say. "Straiya should be up above us all, blowing with the wind."

The room grew quiet. I pictured the world Leyren built with their words—the world we'd almost forgotten, one that lingered along the edge of our memories.

"You're giving out false hope and you know it. That's not the world that waits for us. There is a lot of death out there for us to take from, but it's not a good kind of death. It's destructive. You think there's fruit out there for Rhyse? You think Straiya will be able to fly the moment she steps outside these walls?" Ighta stood. "Face it, Leyren. You don't know what you're asking us to do."

"I do know, Ighta. I know that we will *die* if we don't leave this place soon. Turr is *begging* us to leave. Don't you see that wall? Don't you realize she's showing us how she's going to spread over the lab and return it to her body?" Leyren shook with energy, or maybe rage.

More than likely, it was a mix of both.

"Turr has called us. I felt it this morning, so did Clyra, and I won't let us ignore that call. We have to leave and we have to leave soon." Leyren glared at us, daring us to contradict them.

"I would like to try," Straiya said. "I know I'm not going to get my flight back as soon as I leave, but I think I can work on it. Turr isn't going to abandon us. She's going to help us heal. I don't know if I'll ever fly as easily as I once did, but maybe my feet will leave the ground for just a few moments, and that will be more than enough." At the thought of flying, her body lit up, the strands around her face dancing.

"And what if we get worse? Look at me." Ighta gestured at their body. The sores had only grown, weeping wounds mixing with secreted poison and running in rivers down their skin. "You think I'd survive for long out there?"

"Turr takes care of us in life and death." The saying seared across my mind, so vivid I could almost hold them in my hands. They were our reminder that Turr was always with us. Back when we'd lived freely every day, we didn't fear death. We knew it was part of the journey of life, and that, even in death, Turr would take care of us until we returned to life.

"Some cute little saying doesn't change the fact that I'm dying," Ighta growled.

Yori held out their hands. "Please, Ighta, let us help you. Let us give you hope. Turr will take care of you. She is trying to care for you now."

"You don't want to touch me. I'm disgusting."

My soul ached, watching them wither before our eyes. I'd said something so similar to Leyren not too long ago, feeling so gross in my own skin that I couldn't bear to pass it on to someone else. But Ighta couldn't handle this on their own, and they had to know they didn't have to.

"I do want to touch you." Yori's eyes filled with tears. "Please, just take my hand."

Ighta froze. I tried to step forward, but Leyren

held me back. This was not my moment to interrupt. Not my moment to help.

Ighta had to choose to help themself before we could help them.

They reluctantly stretched out a hand. The distance between them and Yori grew smaller. I held my breath as Ighta took a step forward, a sudden desperation filling their face. They were lonely and they felt uncared for.

Right before their fingers brushed, Yori's tracker went off. Violent light scattered across the room. Ighta turned away, the moment soured. Yori stood with uncertainty, shoulders slouched, tears streaking down their face.

Ighta faced the wall. They drew in a deep breath, squaring their shoulders. "I will go," they said finally, "but I do not expect to make it for long. I can only hope that when I die, it won't be in the confines of a human cage."

I felt no victory in hearing them say those words. The hurt, the giving up, the certainty of their death was not something that settled well within me. I rested against Leyren and soaked in the energy tingling between our skin.

We wouldn't know if Ighta was wrong until we left.

INVIDIA

Day 3 Since Humans Made the Dead Zones

Resley's body started crumbling as the darkness spread into him. He pushed his body in front of Invidia, the vines closing around them, protecting them from something—something Invidia couldn't see, something they didn't want to remember.

"Invidia?" Resley's voice startled Invidia from their thoughts. They didn't dare to look at his face. Sometimes when he spoke, his voice seemed to float on the air, disembodied from his lips; other times, only his mouth moved, eyes staring motionless at the path ahead. It frightened Invidia when he spoke, but the silence still frightened them more, along with the possibility of his voice falling silent . . . forever.

"Yes, Resley?"

"Are we there yet?"

Invidia licked their dry lips, dragging one foot in front of the other. Their legs burned and ached, their body heavy with the stale, dry air that lacked the moisture they needed to breathe freely. "I don't know."

"I don't remember the trip taking this long."

"You hardly ever made the trip."

"Maybe *you* just don't remember it taking this long."

A shiver ran down their spine. *How would you know what I do or do not remember?*

"Do you remember much from before the darkness?"

Please be quiet. Please don't talk about that.

"Like the way the waters used to run a dark purple and the waterbug Turrians would dance across the water's surface, and how they built their huts on the lily pads? Do you remember how the lily flowers grew big enough to play hide and seek in?"

Invidia tried to remember. But most of their memories of Turr from before the dark rot had grown hazy, confused, distorted with death. "I don't think I remember anything that hasn't been tainted with rot." Tears danced in their eyes, creating a black fog that marred their view of the dusty world. "Was it ever completely alive? Or has it always been dead, and I've only just realized it?"

His laugh rang through the air, passing through the shimmering green leaves like an ill breeze. "It wasn't always like that. The rot is in your mind, distorting your memories. Not all of them are truly dark. Some are hidden. You just don't want to remember. You've been hiding so many things from yourself, things you are ashamed of, afraid of. Haven't you?"

"Please, let's not talk about this, Resley. Okay?"

The once pretty laugh turned menacing. "Why? Because you're afraid you're losing your mind? Look around you, Invidia? Can you really *see anything?*"

Shaking their head, Invidia squeezed their eyes shut, stopping their trek. "I don't want to look. The sun is setting anyway, and it'll all be dark regardless. Why are you doing this to me? I thought you were my friend?" Finally, they turned to look at his head resting on their shoulder.

He didn't move to meet their gaze.

In fact, he didn't move at all, and neither did his voice speak again. The silence cut deeper than his harsh words.

Taking a deep breath, feeling their cells rasping against the dryness, Invidia continued down the path. *It can't be much longer, right?* From distorted memories, they'd thought they remembered the walk only taking part of a day. But it was nearly impossible to separate memories from nightmares. Had

Isagani ever existed, or was it also another figment of their imagination, just like the green life around them now?

Panic weaved its way up their chest and into their throat, constricting the muscles, leaving Invidia gasping for air between soul-wrenching sobs and soft black tears.

"I don't want to lose my mind. Turr, where are you?" But the only whispers they felt from the planet were of letting go and leaving behind. If Invidia didn't even know where they were headed, how would they know what to leave behind?

Without warning, their tired legs gave out. The ground rushed up much too fast, and before they had time to brace for their fall, their face smashed against the gravelly green moss. Darkness encompassed them.

Two Years Before Humans Made the Dead Zones.

"Invidia, Invidia! Where are you? The game is over. It's time to gather the compost!"

Invidia covered their soft pink lips to muffle a giggle. Hiding from Indigo was far too easy. When footsteps padded down the walkway, Invidia closed their eyes, drew their legs and arms tight around their body, and titled their shroom headcap to the pathway to hide their face. To anyone passing by, they would look exactly like the non-sentient mushrooms around them.

"Come on, Invidia! I'm serious. I've been looking for you for hours, and I'm hungry and tired! Let's go eat." Indigo's dramatic and lethargic voice rang out, a common tone for them as their shroom type induced sleeping. It was natural for psychedelic and sleep-inducing shroompeople to be such good friends; while Indigo didn't have much energy, Invidia had plenty, enough to match their mischievous spirit.

When they saw little blue shroom feet stop in front of them, Invidia jumped onto the pathway and hollered, "Shroooom!"

Indigo yelped and stumbled back, falling into a springy bed of fungus tree saplings. Invidia bent over laughing as they surveyed the look of surprise and shock on Indigo's face.

"Oh Invidia," they whispered quietly as Invidia howled with laughter. "Why do you insist on straining my nerves like that?"

"Because of the look on your face. It's priceless, and more expression than I ever see on you. It's worth it."

Invidia helped pull them to their feet and brushed off little bits of green and orange moss, picking a few of the green fungus saplings from their backside. Already, Indigo's face had sunk back into their puffy, tired

cheeks, making them look still asleep, or just waking up.

"Well I'm an antiseptic shroom, Invidia." They stretched and yawned. "What do you expect?"

But Invidia wasn't looking at Indigo anymore. The color drained from their rosy, pink freckled cheeks, their headcap paling. "Indigo, listen to me. We have to run."

With slurred words, Indigo started to turn, but before they could see what had upset their friend, Invidia grabbed their hand and started running.

Breath burned in Invidia's cells as they ducked under a group of huge purple snapdragon flowers that watched them with solemn eyes, nipping at each other with their dragon-like lips.

"Where are you running to, Invidia? Come play with us." The flowers reached out to the shroompeople, coaxing them back, but Invidia couldn't stop. Couldn't look back. Couldn't save them all.

The air rent open with the sound of a horn—the hunters.

Indigo screamed, their hand breaking from Invidia's as they looked back.

It only took a second—a second for them to be distracted, to be afraid, to trip and fall face first into the baby yellow ferns that mewed when pressed under the shroomperson's weight.

"Indigo! Get up! We have to go!" Invidia stumbled, skidding through the soft topsoil as they turned around and ran back to their friend.

They were too late.

A gleaming metal saw ripped through the snapdragon trees. Screams filled the air before abruptly ending as the human's machine cut the sentient flowers in half.

Invidia couldn't hear themself scream. They ran back to Indigo, attempting to pry them from the ground, pleading for them to move, to run away, to live. But Indigo was frightened. Their body, frozen in terror, betrayed them.

Through the path the saws cut into the baby fern growth, three humans stalked toward them.

"Indigo, please!" Invidia screamed as they pulled on Indigo's arms, hands slick with sweat, eyes blind with tears. "We have to go!"

One of the human's bright blue eyes landed on the two friends. Malice filled his eyes as he pointed to the shroompeople and started shouting orders.

Invidia couldn't stay. They couldn't save their friend.

Small explosions filled the air as nets shot from their cannons. One of the nets snagged Invidia's leg, tripping them. They managed to shake it off before scrambling to their feet.

Indigo's screams chased Invidia far through the fungi forest as they ran and ran and didn't look back, didn't stop running until the screaming had stopped and the engines had driven away.

Then they curled up under the soft arms of a giant, glowing sunset-orange fern and cried until the sky matched its colors and numbness had settled where Invidia's soul had once resided.

Day 4 *Since Humans Made the Dead Zones*

The brightness of the morning sun woke Invidia first. What brought them fully to wakefulness was the throbbing, splitting headache rushing through their sensitive headcap.

Groaning, they touched the top of their cap. When they pulled their hand away, thick, stinking goop clung to their fingers. Nausea welled up inside them as they turned over rough, pale, disfigured fingers. Wiping their hand on a black leaf next to them, they tried to ignore the dizziness swarming over them as they stumbled to their feet.

"Indigo, get up! We have to go!"

Invidia pressed their hands to their face, trying to push the memory from their mind, to bury it where they'd left it last. But now that the memory had re-surfaced, they could do nothing to hide it again.

Invidia couldn't stay. They couldn't save their friend.

Clenching their fists, they swallowed the bitter bile rising against their tongue, trying to quell the wave of sobs clawing its way up their throat. Now was not the time for grief.

When will it be time for grief? a distant voice whispered in the air. **When will you face it and let go?**

Invidia screamed, throwing a black stone into the dead ferns where they thought the voice had come from. The sound of the rock crashing through the crips plants and the stench of rot releasing into the air was their only answer.

"No. There's nothing to face. This is all just a bad dream, a psychedelic illusion. Nothing is dead."

A wave of green washed over the land once again. Color returned to the fungus trees, though some of their broken caps remained scattered across the ground unnaturally.

Invidia sniffed against the tears. They hadn't been able to save Indigo, hadn't been brave enough, strong enough, but that was behind them. The present mattered most right now. Resley wasn't well, and they were saving him. They were taking him back home so the healers could find out what was wrong with him. They were making a difference.

"No one is dead," they whispered as they searched around for their friend.

But he was.

Panic hummed through their cells.

"Resley! Resley! Where are you?" Brushing tears from their eyes, Invidia frantically pushed aside ferns that flickered between yellow and black and snapped off when touched.

"Over here." His voice came unnaturally quiet and full of defeat. Invidia's heart dropped.

Stumbling over their own feet, Invidia rushed to the voice, easily breaking an entire fern bush as they pushed it aside.

"Are you alright?" Invidia crouched next to him and rolled him over.

Half of his face was missing. A lopsided smile drew up his lip. "I don't feel so good, Invidia."

Screaming, Invidia staggered back. They tripped over a rock, and fell, crashing to the ground. Ignoring the new pain in their back and hands, they scrambled away, sobs raking their chest.

Murmurs from Resley filled their air, drifting to Invidia as they drew their legs to their chest, rocking back and forth.

"He's fine. He's alright." Yet the words did nothing to convince themself he was fine, that half of his face hadn't crumbled, leaving a mess of dark red and green on the other side.

"Invidia? Where are you? Are you going to leave me? Please don't leave me."

They wanted to. The realization made them want to retch. They *wanted* to run away, just as they had from Indigo. They *wanted* to never stop running until the plants didn't crackle and turn to dust when they touched them. Until the roots their feet grew while they slept didn't sink into soil devoid of life and nutrients. Until their head no longer ached and their cells no longer sat uneven on top of themselves, tainted with death. Until all of this made sense again.

But they couldn't. They couldn't stop themself from running anywhere but toward him.

"Invidia." A quiet sob escaped his lips as his glazed eyes met theirs. He didn't move to reach for his shroom friend, even as much as his eyes betrayed his desire to. "Thank you. Thank you. Thank you for not leaving me."

Invidia couldn't say a word. They were too afraid

that if they opened their mouth, they'd vomit up the same black rot leaking from Resley's face as they lifted him to a sitting position.

But when they saw his arm lying on the ground instead of being attached to his shoulder, little beetles crawling in and out of the rotting flesh, Invidia couldn't hold it back any longer.

With a cough, bile escaped their lips and splattered on the ground. Invidia screamed. The pain in their chest ached for some sort of release before it ate them like the beetles in Resley. They wished they could shove Resley off them. Their skin crawled as they wondered how many of those beetles crawled in his body right now. Wondered if they crawled in their own body.

"I can't do this," Invidia wailed, shaking and sobbing.

"Don't leave me," Resley pleaded.

Leave him, the wind whispered.

Invidia shook their head. "No, no. I can't leave him. I can't leave him to die."

But he was already dead or dying or every phase of death at once.

With weak, shaking hands, Invidia pulled Resley's stinking body toward them and reached for his arm.

"Thank you," he whispered onto their neck. A shiver ran across their skin.

Invidia didn't answer him. Instead, they quickly stuffed his arm into their dried bag and staggered to their feet, nearly crumbling under his weight.

"We're almost home, almost home," they cried softly as they made their way, one foot after the other, down the winding path once more.

Each time they looked up, searching for the human city they used to remember seeing in the distance, a dark haze covered the sky. Then everything would turn black again. With the blackness came confusion, chaos, and reality—a reality which told Invidia that just as they'd abandoned Indigo for dead in the human's grasp, so had they abandoned Isagani to whatever horror the humans left in their exodus from Turr.

Just like how they'd buried the memory of Indigo, so they desperately wanted to forget what had truly happened to Resley, what had happened to the rest of their friends and their home.

But as they finally reached the top of the last hill, as they finally looked out across the small valley where Isagani had once thrived, Invidia couldn't lie to themself any longer.

The planet was dying.

CLYRA

Day 5 Since the Humans Left

We filled the entrance of the lab, pressed skin to skin, desperate for the comfort we found in each other.

A fresh world faced us. It had rained again, and with each rain, Turr grew cleaner. The ground no longer lay stained black, and the puddles shone, almost clean. Sunlight sliced through the water, specks of dust spinning endlessly in their own little galaxies.

I looked back into the lab one last time. I didn't plan on missing this place, but I didn't want to forget it either. The lobby had taken on a life of its own. More plants had sprouted, fed by the decaying bodies. A large ring of mushrooms sprouted in a circle around the place where I'd fed with Leyren.

"This is it," Leyren breathed. Their eyes glowed with the vicious hunger for complete freedom. "I think we should hold hands." They held their hand out, palm up. I slid my left hand into theirs and offered my other to Rhyse.

They'd all been outside of the lab already. During the rains, they'd danced on the ground, screaming for joy. During the days, they'd searched for food and explored the areas around the lab.

I'd been too scared. Something about the vast *bigness* of this place sent shivers through my body.

But now there was no time to think. They moved forward, pulling me out with them. I closed my eyes until I felt my feet sink into the soft ground.

As one, Turr reclaimed us.

Nervous laughter bubbled inside me. I'd expected this to be a bigger deal. I'd almost hoped this step would tilt our sideways world back into its proper position. But the shift I felt was small. Just a tiny nudge toward normalcy. This calm surety of belonging was the most comforting thing I'd ever felt.

"You all feel that, right?" I looked at the others. They didn't ask for clarification because they knew what I felt—a coaxing in our hearts and a deeper connection within our souls.

We'd barely made it out when the lab began to groan. We ran, pulling each other forward, shrieking and laughing. We leaped across the soft ground until we stood a safe distance away. I turned and watched as Turr ripped away her roots, destabilizing the building. The walls crumbled in on each themselves, the creeping plants finally facing the sun. This memorial of rubble would become overgrown by the forest and a part of the planet's history.

A light drizzle swept through the trees. It turned

the air white, thick mist coating our skin. So much rain had fallen the past couple days, the ground bloated with it, the soil rising as rivers worked their way beneath the surface. My feet sank into the warm mud. This small embrace from Turr felt good.

A cold wind dragged us back to reality. We no longer had the walls of the lab to protect us. We'd stepped back into the wild, back where we belonged. As exciting as this was, we would have to find our own way now.

"We're out. What next?" Ighta waited for one of us to lead the way.

"I don't know. I guess I thought Turr would tell us where to go." I looked to Leyren.

They shrugged. "We could just walk. We'll end up somewhere."

"Somewhere? That's your big plan? We wander around until we end up somewhere?" Ighta scoffed. "I don't know why I followed you out here."

"You could've stayed and seen how that would've worked out for you." Leyren gestured back toward the collapsed lab.

Their voices grew higher as they yelled back and forth. I stepped back, an unsettling feeling creeping through me. The sounds of my body grew louder, drowning out the world, drowning out my thoughts. In the chaos of my own skin, I watched as Straiya's skin began to **slip. It melted, sloughing off in one big piece. Beneath it lay a familiar figure—the shroomperson I'd seen before.**

They didn't look any better now than they had before. They still held a corpse of some unrecognizable creature. The desperation in the way they held onto it sent cracks through my heart.

"I need your help. I need to know how to get to you." I wanted to approach them, but as usual, I remained stuck. The visions always fought against me.

"Follow the river, pass through the city, walk into the arms of death."

I frowned. "Is that where you are? The arms of death?" It seemed fitting.

"Follow the river. The river. Is there still a river?" They placed a gentle hand on the body they held and the head turned to look at me. It opened its mouth.

"Clyra!"

I screamed. Straiya grabbed onto me and kept me from falling onto my back.

"Are you alright?" She made sure I stood steadily before removing her hand.

"I . . ." The others watched me carefully. "I just had a vision. We have to find the river and follow it to the city."

"We're leaving the lab and heading to the city?" Ighta snorted. "What's the point? We'd trade one cage for another."

I didn't have a response for them. The vision shook me more than I cared to admit. Watching the skin slide off Turr to reveal a dying creature wasn't easy.

Turr had to give me more courage if I was to keep experiencing these visions.

"If this is where Turr is directing us, we'd better listen."

A river. *The* river. We'd know it when we heard it. If I paused and listened carefully, all I heard was the rain.

"Do you think we can reach the city before nightfall?" Yori cast a wary glance at the world around us. "I don't know how I feel about sleeping out in the open."

I knew what they meant. I felt like an alien on my own planet. As we walked beneath the trees, their canopies mixing with the large fungi, everything felt too new. Too different. Too much space extended around us with not enough life to fill it.

"I guess there's only one way to find out," Rhyse said brightly. "But if we don't make it, we'll be fine. We were made for this place."

We continued in a tight group, wary of getting lost, yet knowing that even if we did, we were still at home, for all this unfamiliar place *was* our home. I took comfort in knowing Turr rested beneath each step we took.

I'd forgotten how much it hurt to move around. It was a good pain, but pain nonetheless. I held onto my side, breathing heavily. I could feel my insides slowly tearing with each step, could feel the way my body rebelled, falling apart even when I should be getting better. Each mouthful of air stabbed the back of my throat. I tossed my head back and glared at the sky.

"Are you okay?" Rhyse asked.

"My body hates me," I groaned. "I'm not used to this much walking."

He stopped me with a gentle hand on my shoulder. "Don't push yourself too much. You'll get your strength back."

"I want to be comfortable in this world. It doesn't feel right to finally be free of the lab, yet still feel out of place."

"We're adjusting. It's going to take time." He turned and stopped the others. "We need to take a break. We don't want to run out of energy."

I slumped to the ground. Even sitting in the mud felt better than continuing on.

Straiya settled beside me. "You look like death," she teased.

I sputtered. "Thanks. You don't look much better." I lied, jealous of how at home she looked.

She grinned.

"When did you get so serious?"

"Since every breath started feeling like a needle." I shuddered, silence extending between us as horrible memories of needles filled my mind.

"You need to fall back in love with moving." She sank her hands into the mud and splashed some in my direction. "Come on. Get up."

"Straiya," I groaned.

"None of that. Get up!" She grabbed my arm, mud smearing across my skin, and pulled me to my feet. "Move. Get your body used to it." She spun around, graceful and gorgeous. I watched in awe.

"What's she doing?" Leyren came up behind me and leaned against my back.

"Trying to get me to move again. She thinks my body will hurt less if I . . . spin?"

Leyren giggled. "Have you tried it?"

I shook my head.

"Well, come on then." They took my hand and we spun, pushing and pulling as the motion grabbed hold of us. Mud splashed up our legs as we moved faster and faster.

Leyren's hands slipped from mine and we both tumbled back, landing on the ground. I laid on my back and laughed, not noticing the pain as much.

"Now we need to run," Straiya said. She pulled Leyren up, then turned to me. The others watched us.

"*Run?*" I wiped rain out of my eyes. I couldn't remember the last time I'd run without being fuelled by fear.

She took my hand and pulled me forward, ignoring the way I dug my feet into the ground. "Your body has to get used to moving again. Come! Live! Run!"

I grabbed Leyren's hand and we took off, picking up the pace to keep up with Straiya. She let out a feral scream and we echoed it. It felt good to make our way beneath mushroom canopies and slide over mossy ground. We were out of sight of the others, tearing our way across Turr, the whole world ahead of us.

After a couple minutes, Straiya stopped and bent over, panting. "Do you feel better?" she asked between gasps.

I didn't know how to respond. I kept gulping air like I'd never breathed before. Though the pain persisted, it didn't bite as hard. Or maybe I just didn't care as much. It was the pain of living, and it felt beautiful.

I heard my cells rushing in my ears. I bent to clear my head, then realized the sound came from something much bigger than myself. The more I focused on it, the louder it grew.

I didn't know my body very well, but I knew it couldn't thunder like that.

"Is that . . .?" I broke off, too scared to say the words.

"A river?" Straiya finished for me.

Though I'd just stopped running, I dashed forward again, letting the sound guide me through the forest. The aching need to see Turr's water consumed me. I had to know that death hadn't tainted every part of her skin.

The ground came to an end suddenly. A wall of ferns hid a steep drop. Leyren shouted a warning and grabbed my shoulders, pulling me back as the rocks crumbled beneath my feet. I was too startled to even scream. I stumbled back and landed on hard ground.

The others caught up. I crawled to the edge and looked over, determined to see what I'd come here for. Water fell from the top of the rocks and splashed its way to a roaring river below. The water rushed forth, a healthy purple color, which meant the algae still thrived. No black staining, death, or decay could be seen, just a body of water making its way across Turr's body.

"We're going to be okay," I said, pushing myself up. Rhyse grabbed my arm and steadied me. I still shook from almost falling in. "Turr is going to be okay."

I couldn't believe it. I had to back away and let the water leave my sight. When we'd left the lab that morning, part of me didn't think we'd make it. I'd thought the world would be dead and unlivable. Instead, it welcomed us.

I stood alone beneath a fungus tree and let the joyful tears flow.

With dusk came my fear of the dark. During the afternoon, we'd stayed spread out, following the sounds of the river. As the world lost its light, we subconsciously migrated back into a tight-knit group.

The forest made me jumpy. The noises echoed louder and scarier in the dark. Rhyse kept looking around, cautious and alert.

"Did you hear something?" I followed his eyes to the trees and fungi around us. My skin gave the space around me a bit of light, but wasn't bright enough to make much of a difference. If anything, it made me a target.

He shook his head. "I'm not sure. I guess I'm just a little nervous about being out here."

At least I wasn't the only one scared. I hadn't always been afraid of the dark, but night in the lab had been unbearable. We'd fall asleep knowing that at any moment, humans could pour into our rooms and drag us out for tests. In the days after the exodus, I'd grown accustomed to my friends' company during the night.

"I know we're probably safe, but I don't like all this openness." I shivered, hugging my arms to my chest. The wind had become bitter again. "We can't control what's around us."

All of Turr surrounded us, every bit of her wild, caring self. But not even she could guarantee protection, not always. The human invasion made me realize that even planets can be victims.

"I keep telling myself that since we survived the humans, we can survive anything. Turr was a safe place before them, but now we look at her in fear because of how monstrous the humans were. But, we overcame them. Anything else we face will seem small," Rhyse said.

I liked the confidence in his words. He was right. The humans had prepared us to face anything the universe might throw at us. "I guess that's one way of looking at it."

A strange sound split through the night.

We paused, anxious silence boiling between us. I strained to hear it again. It sounded like a rapid clicking that echoed between the trees. I couldn't imagine what kind of monster created that sound.

Was this where we'd die?

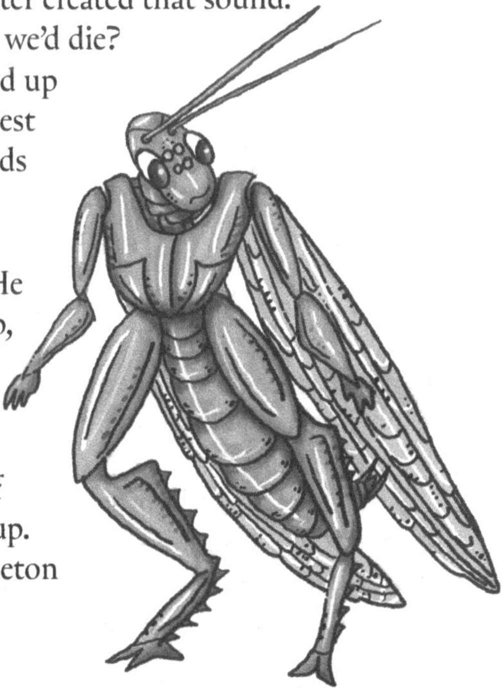

Rhyse scrambled up the side of the nearest fungi tree. His hands buried themselves in the soft white flesh of the stem. He climbed halfway up, then leaned out to look ahead. I watched, eyes wide, as the base of his throat opened up. Behind the exoskeleton stretched a dark cavity. The same clicking sound burst out, spreading through the night.

Another call responded.

He answered again, then dropped back to the ground. "It appears we're not as alone as we feared." He practically glowed with excitement. "Come on, we have to go!"

Rhyse urged us forward. The clicks still rang around us. I had to admit, being immersed in this sort of song was exhilarating. It was a current flowing over the face of Turr, a current that would sweep us up and bring us home.

The underbrush grew thick. Plants grabbed at us, and large leaves slapped against our legs. They dripped, wet with rain. I relished the water as it soaked into my skin. The ground steepened beneath us, the plants giving way to trees and vines.

Rhyse arrived at the top of the hill first. He stopped, taking in whatever lay on the other side. I clambered up next to him. The forest came to an abrupt stop. While the trees around us reminded us of Turr's presence, the space before us represented her vacancy. The skeleton of the humans' city rose before us. I recognized their cruelty. They'd chosen to flatten parts of the planet for their city instead of integrating it with the forest. The uniform structures looked out of place.

In the fading light, I saw the way the plants gripped the buildings, working on tearing them down. Even here, Turr displayed her strength. I wiped tears out of the corners of my eyes. This city would not fade as quickly as the lab. It would be a reminder on Turr's skin for many years. Perhaps it would even become a permanent scar.

But Turr had fought. She became an example. Even if the city wouldn't disappear altogether, she could break it into something smaller.

"Is the city part of the dead zone?" Yori asked.

I shook my head. "The place I saw was still in the wild. It wasn't this." But I knew the city stood between us and the dead zone. We were getting closer.

Dread climbed up my chest, swallowing me from the inside out. I struggled to breathe. We'd left the lab behind, but now faced an even bigger remnant of the humans. The journey was becoming exhausting. No matter how far we ran, we wouldn't be able to escape the monstrosities they'd created. Everything around us stood as a testimony to their destruction.

The city loomed intimidatingly, unfamiliar in ways the planet wasn't. While we had primal instincts to care for us out here, we didn't know how to navigate a world not built for us.

The clicking picked up again. Whoever lived in the city welcomed us in, reminding us that we weren't alone.

"The vision said we had to go through the city," I recalled. "This is part of the journey."

Still, we hung back, wary of this strange new place.

Rhyse moved first. Hesitantly, we followed, detaching ourselves from the forest and giving ourselves back to a place built by humans.

INVIDIA

Invidia staggered down the path. They didn't know why their body kept moving, kept living, when everything else around them remained so very still, so very dead. All the green, red, blue, purple colors they'd wished upon the land had dried up and washed away once and for all.

Black land stretched before them like a never-ending sea of shadow and death.

Huge daffodil stalks, broken off with jagged, ugly marks, stood solemnly across the far side of Isagani. Dried, black petals lay scattered across the ground at the base of the flowers, suffocating what little mushrooms had tried to survive on the rotting plants. The large swampland and river, which had once flowed through the center of the city with clear purple water, now lay stagnant and full of slimy, black rot and dark green algae that took more than it gave.

Fungus trees bent low to the ground. Black veins of death had spread through their once multicolored caps and stalks, puncturing holes of rot inside their forms as black goop ran from scars that refused to heal.

The divisions between each individual garden were long destroyed. Mutations of mushrooms, vines, ferns, bushes, flowers, and other non-sentient plants stood sporadically across the land, some larger than others. All grew colorless or dull with black veins under their skin as they drank poisoned water.

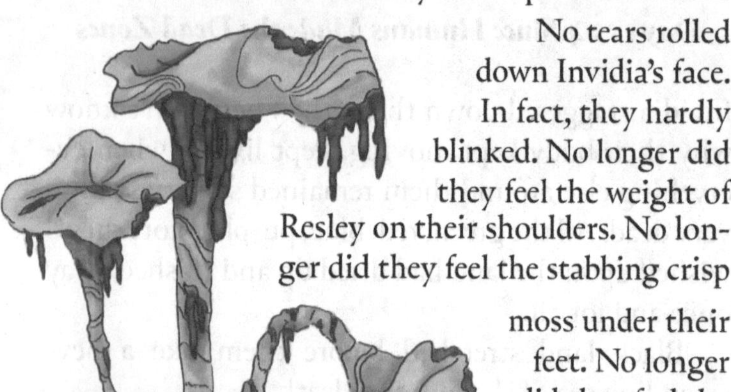

No tears rolled down Invidia's face. In fact, they hardly blinked. No longer did they feel the weight of Resley on their shoulders. No longer did they feel the stabbing crisp moss under their feet. No longer did they feel the throbbing in their headcap.

They felt only the numbness of death spreading through their body, consuming their soul and mind.

With dull eyes, Invidia gazed down at the little mushrooms dotting the ground. Some of them had quiet little faces, eyes closed, looking almost as if asleep. Invidia bent to pick one up, hoping it would jump awake, laugh, and run away. But the entire back half of the little shroombaby's headcap had been caved in. A beetle crawled out of it and dropped to the ground, quickly hiding under the body of another shroombaby.

Moving as if they no longer controlled their own body, Invidia scooped up all the little bodies and gently placed them into their bag on top of Resley's arm.

I need to drop them off before I find any more. I need to make a plan if I'm going to save them all.

Tripping over the weight of their own feet, Invidia stumbled through the once moss and dirt paths of Isagani. Bodies of flying Turrians hung quietly on the broken branches of the daffodil trees, or in circles of splattered and crusted fleshy fluids on top of the fungus trees. Some lay mangled in pieces on the ground.

But every one of them turned their eyes to Invidia, whispering, "Don't leave us. Save us."

Invidia swallowed, their words scratching their unbelievably dry mouth. "I'm coming back," they whispered, choking against the emotions and panic rising in their throat. "Just be patient."

But the cacophony of rasping, crying voices only rang louder in Invidia's ears, pounding against their skull, driving deeper the pain that had already found home in their spirit.

Stumbling through the roads out of instinct—now that all landmarks lay completely unrecognizable—Invidia found themself standing before a pile of dull white vines, suffocated by black veins.

Bending down, they grasped a handful of the vines and watched as the plants dissolved into powder, drifted to the ground, and disappeared into the dry soil. This was all that remained of their home.

Tears once hopelessly buried in numbness now rose unbridled. All the other Turrians' crying silenced, leaving Invidia alone in the stale air. Alone with their thoughts, their emotions, their pain.

Setting down their bag, Invidia let Resley's heavy body slide to the ground before they walked into the desecrated mushroom cave.

The once strong dirt walls, packed tight with dark, nutritious soil, had collapsed, crushing a ring of shrooms in its descruction. Scorching sunlight blazed through the damaged atmosphere, making the enviornment nearly unfit to grow new mushrooms.

When Invidia drew closer, their eyes beheld a sight that rotted their soul with grief. Out of the dozens of shrooms, ten or so had started growing pudgy little cheeks under puffy little caps, covering closed eyes that never got the chance to open.

Turr had blessed them with the unique life. Invidia could've been a shroomparent. They could've been called Dama.

Sobbing, Invidia fell to the ground, ignoring the sharp rocks digging into their knees. With tender hands, they gathered the shroombabies, holding as many as they could in their arms. Some didn't even have their own arms yet. They'd never get the chance to open their eyes, to lift their arms to hug their shroomparent, to move their little legs and run throughout the beautiful garden city of Isagani, lcarning all they could about the once beautiful planet of Turr.

Invidia lay down, curling around the shroombabies' bodies as if even now they could protect them.

But it was too late.

They hadn't been able to protect any of them.

"Don't cry, Dama."

Invidia sniffed, trying to dry their eyes, but to no avail. The black tears seemed to never end. Invidia didn't know how they *could* have an end, not when the black hole opening inside them didn't end either.

"I can't stop."

One of the shroombabies opened their eyes, little arms forming at their sides as they reached for Invidia's shallow face. "You have to stop crying, Dama. They need you." The little shroombaby pointed through what used to be the fungus garden's doorway to the heart of Isagani's ruins, where all the other bodies lay, moaning and calling for Invidia's help.

Invidia shut their eyes, begging Turr to close their ears against the horrific cries. "I can't help any of you. I've never been able to. I'm . . . worthless."

The shroombaby cried and threw itself at its shroomparent, little sobs filling the air, drowning out the others. "No! If it weren't for you, I wouldn't be alive!"

Pain and anger welled up in Invidia's chest like a raging beast. "But you're not—" The words caught in their throat before they forced them out anyway, though it felt like they were ripping their guts out with them. "I'm not sure you *are* alive." The words tasted like poison on their lips.

The shroombaby looked confused as it drew away. "You can't leave us. You can't leave us to rot. You have to save us. You have to *try*."

Let them go. The voice on the small breeze whispered quietly enough for Invidia to ignore.

Pushing to their feet, Invidia took a deep breath of the tainted air, wondering if they even remembered what fresh air smelled like. The shroombaby lay still on the ground, eyes following Invidia.

"I'll wait here," they whispered.

Invidia bit their lip, nodding. Stepping unsurely, they grabbed their bag and moved as far back into the compost cave as they could, trying to ignore the dark mass leaning against the wall outside, not ever wanting to hear Resleys's rasping voice again, but also terrified they wouldn't.

One by one, they unpacked the bodies of the shroombabies they'd saved. The babies remained motionless except for their eyes and disembodied voices. Invidia leaned them against each other, burying their little stems in the dirt so they could stand. With quick hands working almost subconsciously, Invidia cleared out the dead, non-sentient mushrooms and chopped them into easily compostable material to scatter at the base of the shroombabies.

"Is that enough food for now? I know—" They shook their head as they ran their fingers through the powdery dirt, tears brimming in their eyes as they remembered how heavy and moist the soil had once been.

"It's enough … for now," one of the little shrooms whispered before yawning and closing their eyes. They looked unnaturally still standing there, the back half of their blackened headcap missing.

"Okay, okay." Invidia nodded, taking several deep

breaths, mentally making a list of all the things they needed to do. They would have to rebuild the walls around the shrooms—direct sunlight could be deadly to shroombabies.

But in order to do that, they'd need water to rehydrate the soil. That meant going outside of their mushroom garden, walking past Resley, and dealing with . . .

Before the overwhelming pressure could crush them, Invidia stepped outside the room.

The air fell deathly silent. None of the bodies moved. None asked for help.

The silence became worse than the screaming.

"Invidia?" Resley's croaking, distorted voice floated up to them.

Trying to quell the nausea churning through their flesh, Invidia turned to him.

More of his face had crumbled away, but the black goop didn't leak as much from his wounds anymore. His arm, however, still remained very absent. The weight of him driving silent screams through their weak arms, they propped him up against the wall. Then, without a word, Invidia pulled the disembodied arm from the bag, gagging when their fingers sank into the slimy flesh and a little bug crawled over their finger.

With quick fingers, they pressed the limb back against his shoulder, but had to prop it up on the compost box by the doorway.

Knowing they'd need the compost box functional again, and sooner rather than later if they wanted to renourish the soil for the shroombabies, Invidia was faced with the necessity of finding another way to reattach Resley's arm.

"Does it hurt?" They couldn't meet his milky gaze.

"No. I don't think so. Maybe it would've . . . a long time ago. But nothing . . . nothing really hurts now."

Finally, Invidia forced their gaze to meet their friend's one remaining eye. "I'm sorry. For everything." Gingerly, they touched him, letting their skinny hand brush across his slimy, blackened face, trying to remember when his skin had been as green as the vines he'd grown, trying to remember when he'd been whole enough to wink.

"Why?" His eye slipped shut as what remained of his lip curved up. "You didn't leave me behind." Then his eye closed and his head sagged forward into their palm.

Biting their lip until they tasted their own rot, Invidia slowly moved their hand, lowering his head to his chest. "Okay. Okay, you just rest now. You just rest."

But he looked too still to be just resting.

Straightening their shoulders, they took to their feet and slung their bag over their shoulder, ignoring the way the strap crumbled, nearly breaking.

"Just keep breathing, Invidia. You can do this. You can rebuild what you've lost." They ignored the overwhelming wave of uncertainty crashing over them as their eyes traversed the dark and dead landscape. It didn't seem possible the ruins had once been a thriving garden city full of life and joy.

But it didn't matter how impossible it seemed. Invidia had to face the darkness, had to find a way to bring life back to it. They had no other purpose.

You are **weak, worthless, useless.** *Turr has no use for you if you cannot fight for her.*

They marched to the first body of a small bee creature. One of its wings was missing and a huge black gash in its side gapped open where a piece of metal had embedded through it and into the ground.

After pulling out the metal shard, Invidia picked up the motionless apis Turrian and cradled it in their arms, carrying them back to the makeshift cave. They set the little bee next to Resley, ignoring every breath of wind that begged and pleaded, **Let them go.**

Because if Invidia listened, if they buried the creatures and let them all go, nothing would be left—no purpose, no hope, no companionship. Invidia would be alone and worthless to Turr, the planet they'd once spent their every waking moment serving and caring for. They would have to accept death, and that seemed even more impossible than trying to save everyone.

So even though it made Invidia gag and sob every time they carried a mangled body or gathered severed and smashed body parts of creatures who'd fallen from the sky, they pushed down the revulsion along with the pain, the horror, and the pleading wind.

The planet was dying. Screams filled the air.

CLYRA

Day 5 Since the Humans Left

Walking from the edge of the forest to the outskirts of the city was jarring. Unlike the lab, walls didn't contain the destruction. The line between Turr and the humans blurred uncomfortably.

We walked across what had been a battleground. In the construction of their city, the humans hadn't stopped with simply building on her skin. They'd poured thick layers of rock, suffocating her pores. In some places, her roots had broken through, mixing chunks of rock and soil to create purchase for smaller plants to grow. Much like the lab, layers of sap and mushrooms crept across the tough surfaces, working diligently to eat away the invasive structures.

Rhyse led the way, following the call of whoever lived in the city. He stood taller, an awareness of his old self settling over him. Already he was shifting back into who he was meant to be.

I hoped we'd all find a way to do the same.

"Over there." Rhyse pointed toward movement

in the dark. A creature emerged from the night. Built somewhat similarly to Rhyse, she stood only a bit taller, her exoskeleton boasting more colors along the edges.

"Welcome to the end of the world," she said. "I'm Fleur."

"I'm Rhyse." He stepped forward, holding out his arm. They grabbed each other's forearms and twisted them in a traditional greeting.

"We've been expecting more of you to show up."

"We?" Rhyse inquired.

"There are two of us here right now, but we knew we wouldn't be alone for long. You haven't seen the worst of this place yet. Just wait until it gets brighter. This place was the greatest human achievement on Turr, and our goal was to tear it down."

"We're heading to a dead zone." I stepped into the conversation. "I'm Clyra." I stuck out my arm to greet her, but she didn't take it, struggling to even see us.

In the dark, we almost blended in. In the dark, we were almost normal. Almost.

I caught her pause as she looked at Leyren, then again as she reached Ighta. Her eyes hardened at the sight of our strange forms, broken caps, and open sores. Not even the dark could fully hide our pain.

"What happened to you?" She stepped closer to me, now completely in my light. Leyden reached out and placed a hand on my shoulder. I couldn't tell if it was for my support or theirs.

"We came from a lab," I said carefully.

"All of you from the same one?"

"Yes."

We stood uncomfortably as Fleur circled around us, taking in the pain written across our skin. "What did they do to you?" she whispered, horrified.

I couldn't help the tear that rolled down my cheek. This was the first time our pain had been validated from an outside source.

"We were test subjects. They used us to figure out how to tame the planet." I shuddered. Now that I'd seen Turr's strength and resilience, I knew she wasn't a planet to tame. But after they'd broken our spirits, I'd begun to believe she was.

"Well, they failed. We're taking Turr back." Fleur forced victory into her tone. "You're the first group that's come through here so far."

"What can you tell us about the damage to Turr?" Yori asked.

Fleur shrugged. "I don't think even Turr knows the extent of the damage. The city and the dead zones are the big things. Everything else is small in comparison. We just have to hope that if we work together, we can heal Turr and ourselves." Her eyes lingered on our strange bodies. She had the same question as us: How was Turr going to restore us?

Rocks scattered behind her and another figure walked out of the dark. Fleur turned, her throat opening to click in greeting. "This is Astrin." She gestured to him.

He reached out an arm to Rhyse, and they exchanged greetings and names.

Fleur caught Astrin up on what we'd said. I was too tired to focus at this point.

"You must be tired from traveling," Fleur said. "We have places you can sleep. Turr isn't tearing down the whole city. Parts of it remain for those who need to transition slowly. Or you can sleep outside. It's up to you."

"I want to sleep outside," I said. It wouldn't feel right to leave the outdoors so soon after escaping the lab.

"I'm so excited to sleep under an open sky." Straiya sighed, holding her hands to her chest. I threw an arm around her shoulder. We trembled with joy and excitement.

Everything we'd endured had led to this moment. From now on, we were free. I'd spend every day living like it, cherishing it.

We followed them farther into the city until we reached a clearing. Thick grass filled the area, surrounding a stone basin full of tepid water.

"This is a good place to sleep. What do you think?"

Fleur walked around it.

I slipped away from Straiya and fell to the ground. My fingers shook as they grabbed clumps of the grass. I let myself fall into it face first, breathing in the scent of life.

"I think this is perfect," Straiya responded. She dropped beside me and placed a hand on my back. I appreciated the comfort as I fought back tears.

"I think the night will be kind. If a storm approaches, I'll make sure you get to shelter." Fleur watched us settle onto the grass.

I rolled onto my back. The entire universe stretched before my eyes, only ending where my vision failed to see.

"Look at that," I sighed.

Straiya lay down beside me. "It has been so long since we've slept under the stars."

Now that I wasn't moving, the pain turned to a light tingling. It spoke of leaving the old behind and starting a new journey. I hadn't known how the day would end when we left the lab this morning. Now I'd grown more comfortable in the wildness of Turr. She'd begun to feel like home again.

The others settled down. Fleur and Astrin left, taking Rhyse with them. I'd noticed his restlessness since scaling the fungus tree. He'd been itching to test his limits. The night swallowed them quickly. Only their excited shrieks and echoing clicks reassured me they stayed close.

Straiya took my hand and turned to look at me. "We did it."

"We did it." I raised my head to make sure everyone else had found somewhere to rest. The intense tiredness dragged me back down. I closed my eyes, sinking into a peaceful abyss.

Bright light startled me, illuminating the veins on the insides of my eyelids. I jerked awake. I felt like I'd just closed my eyes, but I could tell a few hours had passed. The air held a distinct coolness.

Yori slept beside me. Their arm flashed, so violently alien. It cast all sorts of shadows around us, the world eerily coming to life.

Yori groaned, slowly stirring,

"It burns," they moaned, clutching their arm.

I crawled close to them, aware of the others shifting in the dark, and embraced them. With each flash, their body trembled.

Hands pulled me away. I turned, finding Straiya's eyes in the dark. She continued to drag me away. I twisted myself from her arms, determined not to let Yori face this pain on their own.

"Look out," Straiya hissed. In the panic, I'd missed the plants creeping toward Yori.

Yori tensed as they noticed the tender shoots. The plants slowly wrapped themselves around their arm. Their movements slowed, eyes rolling back in their head as they fell limp.

I rushed forward. Yori seemed to have fallen asleep, the gentle rise and fall of their chest a testament to the life still flowing through them.

The plant tightened its grip on Yori. The jagged leaves jogged my memory. It was a nyphern, one of the few plants we had to be careful around. It held a strong paralyzing juice that could knock anyone out for a few hours.

I cradled Yori's head in my lap, leaving their arm on the ground so the nyphern wouldn't touch me. I trusted Turr. Yori's eyes twitched as they mumbled incoherently, all the while the light flashed obnoxiously. The others gathered around. Nobody spoke, too scared of disrupting the moment.

Fascinated horror crept over me like a chill. The plant maneuvered itself to the place where the tracker sat. It rose, grew still, then darted down, burrowing itself in Yori's skin. Dark sap oozed out.

I gasped, closing my eyes as the plant pushed through layers of rubbery flesh.

Someone gagged as sounds of disgust rose from the others. Ignoring them, I tightened my hold on Yori, who needed my support the most.

"What is it doing?" Leyren hissed.

"It's removing the tracker." Straiya knelt beside me, her soft voice full of wonder.

I opened my eyes again. The sap no longer gushed, though it still trickled down their skin. I couldn't imagine the pain of a plant burying itself in my skin. I thought of Leyren and the mushrooms sprouting across their body.

Yori groaned through clenched teeth. Their body

seized, as if coiling before preparing to spring into action. I ran a hand across their forehead, desperate to comfort them.

All at once the plant froze. I waited, holding my breath. It wiggled, then jerked itself back, bringing out a little piece of metal covered in flesh. The light shone even brighter outside of Yori's skin. The plant shook each time the tracker emitted an electric pulse.

Turr wasn't done yet. More plants gathered around Yori's arm. They pulled the wound together. A patch of moss crept across their skin and filled the gash. In a couple minutes, Turr removed the mark of the humans and replaced it with a mark of her own. The plant holding the tracker retreated into the ground.

Yori shuddered in my lap as the rest of the plants left. The sedative would wear off after a couple hours. I shifted them to the ground beside me.

"That was incredible," I whispered, looking at the others.

Leyren was speechless. They hugged their arms around themself. "Do you think Turr will do something like that for all of us?"

A spike of grief shot through my heart. Turr had removed a physical remnant of the humans from Yori, similar to her tearing the metal city from her own skin.

But the rest of us grappled with crumbling mushroom caps, torn skin, and something else. Something inside.

Turr couldn't heal that with a simple plant.

I took Leyren's hands. "We're going to heal. We may never go back to looking like we once did, but Turr will take away our pain." I believed it enough to say it fiercely.

Leyren locked eyes and nodded, a touch of relief crossing their face.

The others slowly drifted off to sleep again. Leyren helped me move Yori. I didn't want them to sleep next to the messy grass. We stayed close by, wanting to be there when they woke.

Yori woke with a cry that wrenched me from my sleep. I had an arm on their shoulder, a cocoon of warmth built between us. They turned, meeting my eyes. Their hand found the moss on their arm and patted it in confusion.

"What happened?" they asked. On the other side of them, Leyren sat up.

"Turr removed the tracker," I whispered.

Yori's eyes filled with tears. Everything they'd suffered at the hands of the humans had been embodied in the tracker. Now, all that pain and fear lay buried in Turr.

I held them. In this unfamiliar world, we had to be closer than ever before. We'd come to learn that we only had each other and Turr. Even when we were separated, even when we were hurt, we always came back to the point where we took care of each other.

INVIDIA

5 Years Ago When the Humans First Landed

"Invidia! Come look! The stars are falling!" A squeaky voice pierced the air from further down the path.

Invidia giggled as they tripped over a little ring of mushrooms and fell into a springy mat of moss. "Wait up, Lowen!"

The other shroomperson crashed into Invidia as they stood, sending both of them tumbling into the patch of mushrooms. Their laughter filled the crisp, cold morning air, mingling with the buzzing of large honeybees and their shepherds—apis Turrians.

"Lowen, you're so heavy!" With a shove, Invidia rid themself of their sibling's giggling and squirming body. Lowen had been cultivated from their dama's second shroom growth—the one just after Invidia, but already the younger shroomperson had grown twice as thick as Invidia, who already wasn't a skinny shroom by any means.

A soft hand appeared just under Invidia's headcap. They took it, letting themself be pulled to their feet. Hand in hand, the shroom siblings rushed down the road. Their laughter filled the air, accompanying their outlandish theories as to why stars were falling.

Even in the dazzling morning light, the trails of fire behind the plummeting masses shone brightly.

"What if they're not stars?" Invidia whispered. With a grunt, they scrambled onto the top of a short fungus tree and reached back to help Lowen. Then they boosted their sibling onto the next tallest, before bouncing up behind them.

"Well, what else would they be?" Lowen planted their hands on their soft hips, grinning at Invidia as they struggled to climb onto the last fungus tree.

"I don't know." Invidia pulled themself onto the glittery purple shroomcap—one big enough to comfortably fit twenty shroompeople. From here, they could look down into Isagani and see its full expanse from one hillside to another, nestled tightly in the valley they called home. Daffodil and fungi forests dominated most of the landscape, the flowers and fungus providing much needed shade for the land below. Between them grew snapdragon and fern forests, many of which possessed the unique, sentient life of Turrians.

Squinting against the morning sun, Invidia spotted the wasp nests built in the fern branches. Hollering, they waved, hoping Lorna would see them.

A shout rang from below. Invidia watched happily as Lorna kissed her parents goodbye and rushed toward the fungus trees Lowen and Invidia had climbed up. Lorna had just transitioned from larvae to adult form and still wasn't quite used to her wings enough to fly directly to the top of the fungus trees. Even so, she was learning quickly, and Invidia held full confidence her friend would be helping pollinate the daffodil and snapdragon forests right along with the butter-flies, wasps, bees, and dragonflies before the heat of summer faded.

"Invidia, look!" Lowen poked Invidia's arm until they turned to see what gained their sibling's attention.

"Great flower of Turr," Invidia whispered, their mouth dropping open, eyes fixated on a particularly large ball of fire racing from the skies. It collided with the surface of Turr just on the other side of the valley's hill.

A blinding flash of white light exploded from the impact. For a breathtaking moment, everything fell silent.

Then a boom rushed across the land, bending daffodil and fungi trees in its wake. It hit Invidia, knocking them to the side of the fungus' cap. Unable to hear their own scream over the ear-splitting roar, Invidia flailed blindly, struggling to gain purchase on the fungus' smooth cap and slow their fall.

A little hand grasped theirs and pulled. Their shoulder ached with a sudden jolt of pain as their fall halted abruptly. Digging their fingers into the soft flesh of the fungus, they pulled at the same time as Lowen. With a cry of effort and Lowen's dedicated help, they managed to get Invidia back on the fungus' cap. But the once breathtaking sight that had greeted them from their vantage point had morphed into a waking nightmare.

Screams filled the air. Countless daffodil and fungi trees lay snapped in half, some even shredded from the blast. Sticky sap oozed from their woods, glinting eerily in the light. The closer to the hills, the more damage ravished the land.

"Invidia! Lowen! Why are you still up there?"

Vaguely, Invidia heard the voice calling to them. They couldn't focus on it. Their head rang. Their ears oozed a sticky liquid down their neck. The world spun.

"More are falling! We have to run!"

Lorna's words didn't make sense until Invidia and Lowen looked at the sky. Another ball of fire streaked toward them. Straight toward them.

The reality of the situation hit Invidia all at once. Without another moment's hesitation, they grabbed Lowen's hand and leaped off the fungus cap. They hit the next cap hard and their legs collapsed. They tumbled to the next, then the next, until the ground rushed up to meet them. Even with the softness of the moss, Invidia still knew their rosy flesh would be colorful with bruises the next day.

Before they could process anything, Lorna had grabbed both of their hands and started running. After a few seconds, three large wasps reached under their arms and lifted them from the ground. The fungal forest rapidly fell behind them as they were carried from the blast sight.

Invidia tried and failed to look back, to see the star falling from the sky. They could do nothing to hide from its heat just before it hit Turr's skin.

The explosion turned the sky from blue to white, red, and yellow. It burned Invidia's back. It singed the wings of the wasps who'd tried to fly them to safety.

They fell.

Invidia's eyes opened slowly, painfully. The room smelled dark and moist. Turr lay quiet. Unusually quiet.

Invidia groaned as they tried to move, tried to observe their surroundings in the darkness. The last thing they remembered was their descent from the sky just above the purple swamp lands. The clouds behind them had been on fire, the roar of the impact destroying what little had been left of Invidia's hearing. Maybe that's why they couldn't hear Turr.

But as Inivida placed their hand to the soft soil, they knew Turr had truly fallen silent. They couldn't even feel the familiar rumblings of life moving throughout them and the plants.

Staggering to their feet, Invidia patted their way through the darkness until they came to a wall. They then followed it to a small door made from an old daffodil stalk. Pushing against it, they stumbled into the light.

For a moment, they thought fire had eaten the sky again and they were back in the explosion.

Then the flashback cleared, and Invidia found themself standing in the middle of bustling chaos. Shouts rang out around them as creatures ran to and fro, some carrying baskets of plants, others carrying medicinal herbs. In a daze,

Invidia stumbled into the center of the chaos, feeling almost invisible.

Then a voice called out to them. "Invidia! You're awake!" Six hands reached out and brought Invidia into a tight hug.

Tears broke from Invidia's eyes as they wrapped their own arms around Lorna. "What happened? Where is Lowen?"

Lorna pulled away, leading Invidia to a gathering of shroompeople. Invidia knew some of them, but none of them were Lowen. They continued to search for their sibling as they struggled to make sense of what Lorna was telling them.

"They weren't stars. They're some sort of pods from a different planet. There's strange, fleshy creatures who arrived in them that are nothing like us. They're . . . horrifying."

Invidia shook their head. None of this made sense. The chaos around them stirred panic and disorientation inside them. Their ears still rang from the explosions. Tens of colorful shroompeople milled around the gathering, some helping others, some huddled under fungus tree caps, crying. But not one of them possessed the same vivid pink and white ridged cap Lowen shared with Invidia.

"Fleshy creatures? What are they?"

"Aliens of some kind. But they're not plants or insects or mushrooms. They're something else. We've been trying to make contact with them, to find out why they've come here, but so far anyone we've sent to their landing sites haven't returned. Dozens of forests have been wiped out." Tears gathered in Lorna's eyes. "Some of the wasps had homes there. I think . . . I don't think they escaped."

Invidia stopped and turned to their friend. Dread opened inside them like a gaping hole. "What do you mean landing sites? It looked like they crashed."

Lorna's wings buzzed uncomfortably. Invidia winced when they spotted the gapping singe marks in her wings. Her antenna twitched as she blinked her large dark eyes. "No. They landed. It was so violent though. Everything they do feels violent. They've torn open Turr's body to build something . . . with metal."

Nausea washed through Invidia's cells. Sliding to the ground, they hung their head, struggling desperately to come to terms with everything they'd been told. "But the metal, it's . . ." They couldn't bring themself to finish the sentence.

Lorna knelt beside them, tears racing down her exoskeleton. "Turr's bones. I know. Why do you think she's so quiet?"

Invidia couldn't hold back the bile as it escaped their lips. Lorna rubbed their back while they cried and spit out the half decomposed compost.

"Where's Lowen?" Invidia staggered to their feet, shoving Lorna away. They remembered how they'd been lifted into the air by the wasps, only to be thrown from the sky, falling, falling, falling until the swamp waters claimed them. After that, everything had been dark.

"Invidia, they—"

Invidia jumped to their feet, screaming Lowen's name. They raced through the fungus trees, searching everywhere for their sibling, asking any shroomperson who wasn't too lost in their own grief to listen. No one had seen them.

"Lowen!"

"Inividia!" Hands reached out and spun them around. For a brief second, they thought it was their sibling. It wasn't.

"I'm sorry, Invidia, but they didn't survive. Neither did the other wasps who tried to save us. It's just you and me now."

Everything stilled. The world fell silent. In fact, it seemed as if it had stopped all together. Nothing made sense anymore.

"I have to tell Dama. I have to see them." Blind to anything but the overwhelming urge to be surrounded by family, Invidia tried to push past Lorna, but she wrapped her arms around the shroomperson and held them close.

"They—"

Invidia stilled as they heard the tone of Lorna's voice. All hope and purpose drained from their limbs as they sagged against their friend. "No. No. No," they pleaded, but no single word could stop the truth.

"Your shroomparent was one of the first who volunteered to go speak with the aliens. They . . . never came back."

Invidia turned to their friend, searching her face for any sort of truth that didn't hurt. They saw none. Invidia buried her soft face against Lorna's shoulder and wept.

Day 5 Since the Humans Made the Dead Zones

Slowly, Invidia's eyes blinked open. Tears ran down their face as the memory's last images faded. They'd spent the last five years trying to bury these soul-rending memories. But now, too tired to keep up their comforting lies, the horrors of their past spilled forth unbridled.

Darkness filled the air. When they looked past what used to be an arched ceiling of packed moist dirt, now reduced to dust and open air, they hoped to at least see the stars, safe and secure in the great expanse.

But the darkness pressed forward, overwhelming and complete. Whatever dark, dusty haze hung in the air, seeping into the plants and poisoning their veins, also refused to grace the land with starlight.

Shivering, Invidia curled in on themself. They'd never been cold before. Not when they'd been pudgy and round with little rolls of rubbery flesh. Now, hardly anything besides thin, slimy skin sat on their form. The cold crept into them like a disease, waiting for them to close their eyes and succumb.

Against their back, they felt the still form of Resley; to their front lay a wasp creature with a striking resemblance to Lorna. Invidia hadn't been able to find Lorna. Yet. They wondered if she and this wasp had hatched from the same nests and if Lorna had ever started her own family. Vaguely, Invidia remembered Lorna talking about building a nest; she'd picked the perfect daffodil stalk just steps from the center of the wasp pollinator's territory—the perfect place to raise small larvae. Though, Invidia hadn't always been focused during their walks.

Fresh tears filled their eyes. *Actually, I was never*

focused at all when it came to my friendships. At least, not after Indigo . . .

The pain grew too great to bear. But bear it they did, for they could do nothing else.

"Maybe Lorna is out there somewhere, just like I was, trying to get home. Maybe they weren't here when—"

Images of the humans' ships taking to the skies clawed at the back of their mind, striving desperately to overwhelm, overpower, consume, corrupt.

Invidia clenched their eyes shut against the memories they'd tried so hard to forget and hugged themself. Their arms offered little warmth or comfort. Shivering, they pressed against Resley's body, colder than their own.

"Maybe Dama isn't really dead either. Maybe now that the humans are gone, they'll all come home. Maybe Lowen will too."

And though it had been five years since the humans landed on Turr, five years since Invidia had seen either Lowen or their dama, they clung to that hope as sleep descended upon them, no matter how foolish that lie seemed.

CLYRA

Day 6 Since the Humans Left

Cold hands tapped my shoulder. I jerked awake and almost knocked my forehead against Rhyse. He pulled back, surprised.

"Sorry," he said, "I didn't mean to frighten you."

I held a hand to my chest. My soul pulsed against my skin, drumming in my ears. The frigid fear slowly melted away. I couldn't hide the embarrassment flushing across my face. For a moment, I'd thought I was dying.

"It's fine. I overreacted." I shifted, my body rooted to the ground beneath me. I lifted my arm and the roots retracted. "That's new." The roots slithered back into my skin as I pulled myself from the ground.

"It was good for you to sleep out here," Rhyse commented.

"It was." I looked at Yori. They slept on their side, their wounded arm hidden from sight. "Turr took out Yori's tracker last night."

"She did?"

I nodded. "She put Yori to sleep and sent plants

into their arm to pull it out. It was . . . scary and gross and beautiful." I shivered at the memory. I was glad she'd done it while we were half asleep. It felt like a fever dream.

I would hold that memory close for the rest of my life. It was important for me to remember Turr's power.

"I'm sorry I missed that. I would've loved to see it."

"You were off experiencing your own changes. I'm glad you could get out and do something for yourself." I lifted my legs, the last of my roots letting go of Turr. I felt ready to face the day. "Why'd you wake me?"

"Fleur wanted to help us through part of the city. There seems to be quite a storm approaching, and she thought we might like to shelter it out."

Before the humans, Turr didn't have violent storms. I could remember warm rains gently washing over the planet. The way those rains felt, like a full-body hug, was something I desperately wanted to feel again.

So far, Turr's storms had been cold, distant, and harsh.

"Turr didn't used to storm like this."

Rhyse helped me to my feet. "She didn't have to. Rain used to be one of her ways of connecting with us, but now it's a knife she uses to peel human remains from her skin."

Just another way humans changed our planet.

I started waking the others. A gentle tap here, a bigger nudge there, carefully stepping over the roots emerging from their bodies. It seemed we'd all connected with Turr last night.

We had to get moving if we wanted to make any progress. A storm among these unstable ruins could prove dangerous if strong winds dislodged pieces of rubble.

Loud commotion drew my attention. Ighta trembled with rage, their dark eyes flashing a warning to all of us looking in their direction. I didn't catch what had been said, but Ighta seemed angry at all of us. Rhyse said something to them, the wind hiding his words from me. Ighta turned and marched past me, away from the group.

I followed at a distance. If Ighta needed to speak to someone, I wanted to be there. I needed them to know they weren't alone.

"Stop following me," they warned.

I halted mid-step. "If that's what you want."

They spun, their face red with anger. Their skin held a glossy sheen from the infected sores, clear fluids running across them. "Don't," they spit, jabbing a finger at my face. "Don't act nice to me. Don't tell me everything is going to be okay. Don't feed me the same lies you feed everyone else. It might work for them, but I see through it."

"Ighta—"

"I can't *stand* you. You're always saying we're going to be fine, but you don't know *anything*," they screamed. "We're not going to be fine. When will you understand that?" Their voice rose like the wind, bouncing between the buildings. They let out an anguished cry, falling to their knees.

I knelt. "What do you want me to say?"

Ighta stared right through me. "Tell me we're going to die. Tell me this is hopeless."

I shook my head, tears spilling down my cheeks. "I can't say that because I don't believe it."

"Then you're a fool. You and all the others. You think Turr is healing us, but she's just as broken as us. Why didn't she help us before we were tortured? Why didn't she stop the humans from landing in the first place?" Ighta's tone grew bitter. "The answer is that Turr isn't all-powerful. She's a planet who's just as confused as the rest of us, yet we follow her blindly through the dark."

I shuddered at their words. "I don't have answers. I know that Turr didn't leave us because she wanted to. Turr was just as tortured as the rest of us. We're standing on her cracked skin, drinking her life force, and eating the plants she forces through the toxins, yet you don't think she cares?"

Ighta didn't respond. I'd never seen anyone look as helpless and lost as they did right now.

"Did you grow roots last night?"

Ighta bit back a frustrated laugh. "I can't seem to grow roots. My body is too broken to do that. Something you wouldn't understand."

"You don't deserve any of the pain you're feeling,

but we don't deserve your anger because of it. We're trying to help."

"Help someone else. Someone who has a chance. I just need to be alone for a moment."

I lingered in the awkward space between Ighta and everyone else, torn in two directions, empathy straining against my skin. I couldn't help everyone. I couldn't hold everyone's burdens.

But oh how badly I wished I could.

We set off quietly. Fleur showed up on her own as we left our resting place behind. She took the lead with Rhyse, the two of them chatting as we moved.

The city around us felt vacant. It creaked and groaned, roots still working their way through it. Some of the buildings tilted as the ground beneath them heaved.

We didn't see as many dead humans as I'd expected. Those we came across appeared similar to the ones in the labs, their bod-ies falling apart, sinking into the  ground, plants growing in the crevices. I no longer felt any hunger when I looked at them. Turr fed me now, and these bodies were her fuel.

The only dead we stopped to look at, and the only ones the bugs left alone, were Turrians. They lay few and far between.

"Should we be returning them to the forest?" I asked when we came across the third shroomperson. A root tore through its chest, and its large shroom-cap slowly rotted. The sickly stench of decay hung thick around us. I hid my nose in my arm, my eyes watering.

"Don't touch them. They deserve what they got." Astrin spoke from above us. I looked up and spotted him creeping along the side of the building. He blended right in, and I only picked up on him when he moved.

How long had he been watching us?

"What do you mean?"

He dropped to the ground. "Not everyone stayed loyal to Turr. A few figured the humans would take over, and they traded our locations for a place in the city."

My stomach turned at the thought of shroompeople turning in their own kind. Especially knowing what we'd gone through.

"I can't believe they would do that." Rhyse looked at the body in disgust and horror.

"The humans wouldn't have found most of us if they hadn't helped. For an invasive species, they're pretty stupid. I don't think Turr was as similar to their home planet as they'd hoped." Astrin shrugged, a gleam of amusement in his eye. "I guess they didn't expect to find a living planet."

"Is their own planet not alive?"

"From what I've gathered, it seems a lot of planets don't have the same spark Turr has. We're lucky to be here."

Lucky. I snorted. Lucky enough to be on a rich planet with living soil. Lucky enough to get targeted and attacked and dragged from our homes.

But truly lucky that our planet could fight back for us.

"Guys," Straiya warned. She pointed up at the sky. Black clouds boiled along the edge of the city, and the smell of rain swept through the air. I hadn't yet seen a storm this big. Turr was preparing for another cleanse.

"Come on. Fleur found us a place to shelter through it." Astrin's chest loosened and he clicked. Fleur responded almost immediately. Astrin stayed in the front while Rhyse watched the back, herding us away from the imposing clouds.

The storm swept in overhead, and the world turned black as night. We reached the shelter just as the rain began to fall. The winds picked up, the rain like blades on my skin. The drops burned with toxicity from all the foreign liquids draining throughout the city.

We hurried into the bottom of a tower. Fleur led us through a dark area and up some stairs that opened into a hall, rows of open doors lining both sides.

"Every door is a different home. You can spread out, make yourselves comfortable. Just don't travel too far. I don't want to lose any of you." Fleur smiled.

We all walked into the nearest door, choosing to stay together. It didn't feel right to split up. It didn't feel right to be here either. These were the homes of our captors. My stomach turned. Once again we were trapped within the humans' walls.

The humans had been so organized. Every belonging had its place. Their living spaces were small, but neatly packed with odds and ends I didn't understand. How did they thrive within this neatness? What happened when they felt the need to burst beyond the walls?

All at once, I felt suffocated. I left the main room and stepped through a door. A large bed filled most of the space. Sitting on the edge, I focused on breathing. The air felt empty. It didn't fill the craving I had for something fresh.

"Are you okay?" Straiya sat beside me and took my hand.

"I don't want to be back in a place like this." I looked around. The darkness pressed in, the walls squeezing me, pressing tighter and tighter.

Outside, the world *raged*. I could think of no other way to describe it. Turr took every pent up emotion and set it free. Her winds became a scream that crescendoed in my mind—one long note that lasted forever. It cut through my thoughts until all I felt was myself amid Turr's anger.

I tried to speak, but my words wrapped themselves around my tongue.

"Breathe in," Straiya encouraged. She pressed a hand to my chest. I took in a deep breath and let it sit in my lungs.

"Breathe out." She pushed against my chest as I released. We repeated this until I fell back in sync with the cycle of breathing. The room widened and the clenching fist of panic let go of my soul.

"I feel stupid." I got caught between a laugh and a cry, my body shaking. Straiya didn't speak. She just pulled me in and held me until I felt quiet inside.

"You're not stupid. You're scared, and you have every right to be." She wiped my tears away.

We sat in silence until I wanted to head back out to join the others. I searched the room until I found Ighta in the corner. They wiped their skin with a blanket, gently trying to remove the rain from the open wounds, their face twisting with pain.

"They need help," I said to Straiya. She turned and looked at Ighta.

The weight of pain, both my own and everyone else's, had become such a burden.

I grabbed a towel and ran it under the tap. A little water came out, barely soaking through the material. It was better than nothing.

I knelt in front of Ighta. "Do you mind?" I asked, preparing to touch their arm. They watched me carefully, then shook their head.

I washed their skin gently, working the clean water around the wounds. Ighta hissed in pain as I applied more pressure. I stopped. "Am I doing it right?"

"Yeah. It just hurts." They scrubbed their shoulders, their mouth pressed in pain. "It always hurts. The pain is like another skin growing over top of my own. It's the closest companion I've ever had."

Straiya got up and walked away. I looked over my shoulder to make sure she was okay. She held her face in her hands. Being in a human room again made all our pain so much harder to bear. The distraction of freedom couldn't keep it at bay.

"We're going to get you through this. We're your companions, and we'll help you," I assured them.

"I don't deserve it."

"Everyone deserves help. It's not something you have to earn." I worked the water around another sore. Would these ever close? Would Ighta ever shed this pain?

"I'm done fighting, though. I'm going to survive until I stop, and then I'm giving myself over to whatever comes next. I'm too tired to keep going."

I focused on my task. I couldn't stop and think about what they'd just said. It weighed too close to my own soul, feeling too familiar, threatening to pull me down.

When we'd wiped the worst of the damage away, I pulled Ighta in for a quick hug. I couldn't linger because the poison immediately started stinging me, but I put up with it just to let them know how much I cared about them.

"Whatever happens, just know we all care about you."

Ighta turned away, embarrassed by the attention, and retreated emotionally. I set the towel down and left them alone. Like Straiya, I felt a *lot* right now. So much so, I felt I'd drown within myself.

I settled on a chair, the thin padding offering hardly enough comfort. Rhyse dragged another chair, claiming the spot next to mine.

"Are you okay?"

I nodded. "It's a lot, you know? There's always

something happening, always someone hurting. I want to help everyone, but I can't."

"We appreciate it. You're so caring. Just make sure you're not overextending yourself." He leaned back in his chair, the front legs leaving the ground.

"I just feel . . . responsible."

"For?"

"I don't know. Everyone's health? Delivering you all to the dead zone safely?"

"We're all caring for each other. It's not just your job."

"I know."

"I'm worried you *don't* know." He shifted, the chair legs hitting the floor with a thud. His eyes locked on mine. So deep, so full of the complex emotions inside him. "If you pour yourself into everyone else, who will pour themself into you?"

I grinned. "You do, and Leyren does, and the others do more than enough too. I'm fine. Don't worry."

He didn't seem convinced. "I will worry about you until you stop worrying about everyone else." He glanced over at Ighta. He was concerned for them too, and I felt better knowing we were all trying to keep an eye on them.

I sat until I couldn't anymore. I needed to get up and do something. Give myself a little bit of freedom. "Want to explore this building with me?" I asked.

Rhyse didn't answer. He'd fallen asleep, his head nodding on his exoskeleton chestplate. I smiled and left him behind. He deserved a break.

I left the unit and stepped back into the hall. Beside the stairs, at the end of the hall, a large pane of glass stretched from floor to ceiling. I approached slowly. I couldn't see through the white shroud of rain. The wind howled, ripping apart the world.

This was the second face of Turr. She could be calm and loving, caring for those who cared for her, but she was also a wrathful being who would hunt down those who hurt her.

I leaned against the cold glass, pressing my face to it. I saw the ground faintly. Water washed through the streets, staining them black with the toxicity it carried. It looked so different than the world we'd walked through only an hour before.

I lost myself in the storm. It felt good to watch something bigger than myself.

"Her power is terrifying."

I gasped, jerking away from the glass. Leyren stood in the darkness behind me. They hid a laugh. For the second time today, I'd gotten scared for no reason. "It's terrifying, yet comforting."

"The best mix." They stepped up beside me and pressed themself to the glass, just as I'd been. The pale light gave them a ghostly complexion, but they looked better than when we'd been in the lab.

"The cold glass feels so nice." They sighed.

I smiled and leaned against it. After all the stress of the last few years, it felt good to just exist.

"Clyra?"

I met their eyes in the reflection of the glass.

"Yes?"

"Thank you for always trying to take care of others." They smiled. "I need you to know you're appreciated."

I might've cried if I hadn't already been crying a few minutes ago. "Thank you," I choked out. No responses felt appropriate. No words could hold the universe of feelings spinning within me.

"Of course." They stepped away from the glass. "I'm heading back. You coming?"

"I need a few more minutes."

They retreated to the room. In their absence, I turned and sank to the ground, losing myself in the sound of a world tearing itself apart so it could finally put itself back together again.

INVIDIA

Day 6 Since Humans Made the Dead Zones

Invidia woke the next morning to little roots growing from their body and into the dirt for the first time since the humans left Turr. A cry of joy and relief escaped their lips. The roots hadn't grown very deep or strong, and the dirt certainly wasn't nutritious enough to grow any mushrooms, but the feeling of being inside Turr once again filled them with energy and hope. With that hope came a renewed vigor to rebuild.

"No, Invidia. Not there. Over here. It used to be over here." Resley's voice drifted to Invidia as they panted, having just dropped the very heavy compost bucket they'd been carrying.

With a jolt of annoyance, Invidia snapped back at Resley. "Don't you think I know? It's very heavy, and I've never been good at carrying things. None of us shroompeople are."

Weak. Worthless. Useless. They shook their head against the menacing words echoing in their mind and sat on the edge of the compost bucket to steady the dizziness washing over them. "Besides, I don't see *you* helping."

They regretted their words instantly.

Resley whimpered, a tear forming at the corner of his eye. The rest of his nose had fallen away now, reduced to black dust that sank into the slimy rot consuming his chest. "I wish I could, Invidia. I just don't . . . feel very good."

Pain clawed at Invidia's heart as they slumped their shoulders. Some of the enthusiasm they'd woken with died under the compost bucket's weight and the sorrow they'd caused their friend. It wasn't his fault he was . . .

They didn't let themself finish that thought.

"I know. I'm sorry, Resley. I wish you felt better. I wish you were okay." They tried to stem the tears collecting in their eyes. Their headcap sweated and burned under the direct sun, and as sickeningly sweet rot ran down the gilled underside of their headcap, stinging their eyes, they started to cry even more.

Why does this have to be so hard? They looked up to the shriveled dull and black fungus trees. They'd never fully realized just how much shade and protection the fungi had provided. But now they were gone, and just like everything else that had lived and existed in Isagani, Invidia had taken them for granted.

Let it go. Let them go. Whispers on the wind tickled Invidia's cheek, but they ignored it. They couldn't

let go. Not yet. Not when so much still had to be done.

Their eyes landed on Resley, and sorrow filled their heart. Not when so many creatures still counted on them.

Standing back up and forcing oxygen into their cells, Invidia grabbed the handles of the bucket and groaned, lifting it again. "Just a little farther. Just a little farther," they chanted to themself as they staggered to the compost box by the door of their collapsed mushroom cave.

"Do you think that'll be enough?" Resley's weak voice made Invidia want to dump the compost on him.

"I don't know. Probably not. But that's all I could carry."

He stayed silent while they took the lid off and picked up the bucket one last time to dump the dead leaves and plant matter into their compost box. They'd found the full bucket a few fungus gardens down; its lid had protected it from whatever toxins poisoned everything else. It'd seemed so full, so promising when they'd found it—immeasurable progress for them and the other shroompeople they'd saved.

Now it only formed a very small, sad pile at the bottom of a box that once held so much more.

Groaning and sliding down the side of the box, Invidia let their eyes slip shut for just a moment.

Resley's voice woke them again. "I'm really hot, Invidia. Can't I go inside with the others?"

Invidia's body shook with revulsion as their gaze roved over Resley's body. The little pieces of him that hadn't yet been claimed by rot had burned brown from the relentless sun. Invidia also desperately wanted to go inside. The top of their shroomcap reeked of scorched flesh and grew more tender by the moment. They'd be safer under the dead leaves they'd strung across the top of the crumbling walls.

But they couldn't move Resley. Not after what had happened that morning.

"I'm going to move you, okay? I want you to be inside with the others in case it storms or the sun is too hot." Invidia ignored the way Resley's arm sat on the ground by his side. They hadn't yet found a way to reattach it. Truthfully, they weren't sure they'd ever find a way.

"Okay!" Resley sounded happier than he had since they'd found him. But when Invidia went to lift him by reaching under his other arm, the joy dissipated into horror.

Invidia found themself looking at his arm, detached from his body, limp in their hand.

Their screams filled the air.

Invidia shivered against the memory despite the heat of the sun bearing down on them. "I'm sorry, Resley, but you know you can't. You have to stay out here."

Tears gathered in the corner of his eye socket. What remained of his bottom lip quivered. "But I'm so hot."

Anger and frustration escaped Invidia through their tears and sharp words. "I know, Resley, and so am I, but what else can I do? I'm the only one here, and if I don't get more compost, all the shroompeople in there are going to die. I can't do it all!"

"You can't do anything."

Invidia's soul ran cold; they felt as if they'd been slapped in the face. "Resley . . ."

But when they looked at their friend, his head rested heavily against his chest, eye staring at the nothingness in front of him. A beetle crawled out of the empty cavity in his face. They almost left the beetle, left it like he'd left Invidia in their hurt and grief. Instead, they flicked it away.

"Why would you say something like that?"

They received no answer.

Struggling past the weight pressing on their soul and striving to regain some of the joy they'd felt that morning, Invidia finally dragged themself to their feet.

They hated themself for being glad Resley had fallen silent.

With heavy steps, they made their way through marred streets. The city stretched before them, unrecognizable. At first, Invidia had tried to mask the death with green life the way they had days ago, but their veins ran empty of nutrition, their skin burned, their feet bled from the rocks, and the destruction spread too vast to mask with silly illusions and hallucinations.

Though it hurt to see the death, it hurt far less than lying to themself that Isagani still lived.

The planet was dying.

A flash of vibrant dark blue caught the corner of Invidia's vision. Whirling around, heart racing, Invidia tripped over their own feet as they rushed toward the color. A gasp left their lips when they pushed away a slimy fern leaf, revealing a small daffodil tree sapling with a single blue blossom.

For a long moment, Invidia could do nothing but stare and cry. It felt a century since they'd seen such real, vivid color not manifested by their own mind. They didn't believe it until they reached out and cupped the precious blossom in their hand.

Jumping up, they whooped and danced, thanking Turr. "Let's get you home, little flower." They pressed a kiss to its petals.

Racing back to their mushroom garden, they ignored all the creatures calling out to them, grabbed their nearly disintegrated bag, and rushed back to the flower. Then, forcing themself to slow down, they carefully dug around the roots of the daffodil, making sure not to break a single one. Thankfully, the root ball wasn't well established and they easily fit the entire plant and some of the surrounding dirt in their bag.

Not trusting the weak straps, they hugged the flower to their chest, giving it all the support they could spare. Slowly, they trekked back home, making sure to avoid tripping on the jagged metal scraps and rocks.

"What is that, Dama?" A little shroom's voice called to them from inside the mushroom garden. For a moment, Invidia waited for the shroombaby to run out and meet them.

They never did.

With a stab of disappointment and frustration with themself for forgetting the shrooms weren't well enough to move, Invidia stepped into the doorway, proudly displaying the daffodil.

Cheers filled the room.

"Oh thank goodness! I'm so hungry!" Little hands reached out greedily.

Invidia had to hold the daffodil up and away from a butterfly's big blinking eyes and outstretched hands, their long rainbow-colored tongue slipping in and out of their cracked blue lips.

"No! You can't have it just yet! It's hardly big enough to hold itself up, let alone feed you. You'll have to wait until after I plant it and it grows bigger."

The cacophony of protesting pollinators made Invidia's ears ring. For a moment, the ringing turned into a roar, taking Invidia back to the blinding light, the heat of the explosions, the death . . .

An explosion shook the planet. Screams filled the air.

"Everybody! Be quiet!" Invidia's scream pierced the air, echoing in the silence that followed.

Wide, teary eyes watched them fearfully.

"I'm sorry, it's just"—Invidia's body shook—"there's so many of you, and—and there's only one plant, there's only one me, and I just—"

"Wouldn't it be easier if you just let us go?" The young wasp creature sighed heavily, big black eyes reminding Invidia so painfully of Lorna.

Tears poured down their face as they tumbled over their words. "No. I mean, yes, it would. But I'm not—"

The wailing and crying grew louder. "You just want to save yourself! That's all you've ever done!" A little shroombaby pointed accusingly at Invidia; most of its little arm had been reduced to powder from the toxins.

"No, no!" Betrayal ripped through Invidia's chest. "I tried so hard to save them! All of them—Lowen, Dama, Resley, Indigo. I don't know what else I could've done!"

They didn't want to listen, didn't want to face the truth, but the creatures' words stabbed them over and over. Invidia couldn't escape them, even as they ran from the fungus garden.

"You've never been enough! What are you even good for? Nothing!" The spitting voices followed them the whole way.

Invidia screamed against the noise, hardly noticing when they tripped and fell, a chunk of their headcap breaking off when they struck the ground.

Whimpering and curling into themself, Invidia tried to cover their ears, tried to block out the words they didn't want to hear but believed deep down.

"You're not strong enough. You're **weak. Worthless. Useless.** You're not smart enough, not caring enough. **Turr has no use for you if you cannot fight for her.**"

"Please, Turr," Invidia whispered between sobs. "Please help me understand. What am I here for? What is my purpose if I can't protect them? If I can't protect you? Please help me."

A gentle breeze washed over Invidia as the dark of the night descended once more. Dirt reached out, pushed by the breeze, to wrap around the shroomperson's cold, shivering body like a hug.

Trust me, little shroom. I have never left your side. I have a purpose for you, but you must trust me and let them go.

CLYRA

Day 7 Since the Humans Left

I woke in a city split by rivers. The constant sound of rushing water loomed around me in the dim room. I stared at the unfamiliar ceiling, trying to orient myself. A moment passed before the memories came back to me.

Leyren and Straiya lay on the bed next to me. I moved carefully, pushing myself to the edge of the mattress, and rolled off onto the cold floor. The soft sounds of breathing continued unhindered. Satisfied, I left the room.

Yori and Rhyse slept on comfortable chairs. Their blankets had slipped down in the night. I stopped to tuck them back in, then set about looking for Ighta. Though they'd fallen asleep on the floor, only a rumpled blanket remained.

I leaned out of the door and peered down the hall. Ighta stood by the window, their frame silhouetted in the white morning light. The floor creaked when I stepped out.

"Who's there?" they asked. They didn't take their eyes off the city.

"It's Clyra."

"Don't come closer unless you want to see dead bodies," they warned.

Morbid curiosity drew me to the window. I looked down, taking in the layer of water washing over everything. The rivers brought up the dead, bearing the bloated, disfigured shells that once held life.

I didn't feel anything for the humans that washed past. They'd asked for death when they decided to take over a planet. My heart broke a little each time a shroomperson floated by. I could understand the desperation that led them here. In the hopelessness of the humans invasion, some must've felt they only had one choice.

I turned my back on them like they did to us.

These dead deserved no respect.

"What are you doing up so early?" I asked.

Ighta shuddered. "I can't sleep. I'm scared, Clyra." Their voice shook.

"Scared of what?"

"Dying."

The word sucked all the oxygen out of the hall. I rested against the glass and stared into the darkness, searching for the right words.

"What do you think it means to die?" Ighta turned and stared down the hall with me.

"I think death is a cycle. When we die, Turr takes us in, and we become part of something else. Eventually, we regrow and do it all over again."

"So when I die, I'll get to rest?"

I closed my eyes and took a calming breath. I knew where this conversation was going, its ending inevitable. "When you die, Turr will hold you until you're ready to move on."

"I'd like that."

"Ighta—"

"Don't. It's fine. I know what's coming and I just need to be ready for it." They pushed away from the glass. Without support, their weakness was visible. They could hardly stand on their own.

"Do you need help?" I reached out to steady them, but they pushed my hand away.

"Just promise me you won't let me die in the city. I've lost enough to the humans. I refuse to die on their land."

My breath caught. "I promise. We're going to get you out of here." Panic rose like vomit, clawing up the back of my throat. I didn't know how much longer Ighta had, but they seemed to think their end loomed near.

They sank to the ground and stayed there, their will to live draining right before my eyes. We only had a couple hours at best before they succumbed to the warm hands of Turr.

I hurried down the stairwell. The dark consumed me, forcing me to feel my way around. The cold walls had grown slimy with the excessive moisture. My hands slid across the stones.

An inch of water spread across the ground floor. It lapped at the steps, a thick, oily mess reeking of poison and death. I stopped, my feet inches away, and searched for a way out.

Fleur and Astrin roamed the city. Could they find a way to get us out?

I crouched on the bottom step and peered closely at the water. Beneath the murky surface, plants spread like veins, their skin the colors of decay. The edge of one stuck up above the water. I poked it tentatively **and Turr took my hand.**

She pulled, yanking me off the step and into the air. I fell, floated, spinning and screaming and never quite going anywhere. The world no longer possessed reason or rhyme.

I lay, scared, consumed with the overwhelming sense that I wasn't alone.

I twisted, trying to find something else in this new reality. At the center of it all, a black hole engulfed all life, sucking in me, dragging me closer and closer, the gravity compressing me as I approached the end.

I closed my eyes, and it all stopped.

"Clyra," a gentle voice coaxed.

When I looked, the black hole had transformed into the shroomperson. They watched me carefully. Along their body, their skin rotted away, revealing tender insides.

"I need your help."

The words tore me apart. Everyone every-

where needed me. I had to get Ighta out of the city and the others to the dead zone. My responsibilities were endless.

"I'm coming," I whispered. They couldn't hear me.

"Clyra?"

Their lips hadn't moved.

"Clyra, wake up."

Stinging pain, nausea in my stomach, a hand pulling me back to life. I choked and turned, throwing up on the ground.

"Woah." Fleur pulled me up, poisonous water dripping from my body. "What are you doing?" She helped me back to the steps.

I spit, trying to rid my mouth of the sharp taste of rot. "I was trying to find you, but I had a vision." I didn't feel well. The world hadn't settled around me yet.

Fleur worked on wiping the water off me. "You're lucky I found you. Exposure to this water for too long could've caused some real damage."

I looked at my arm. Though the skin was red and irritated, it didn't *hurt*. That's all I cared about. "We need to get out of the city. Ighta is dying and they don't want to die here."

Fleur paused. "Are you sure they're dying?"

I thought back to how they'd looked the last time I saw them. I knew without a doubt they couldn't come back from this. Turr couldn't heal them. The sick water swirling around us was proof enough that

Turr had almost no energy to spare.

"I'm sure."

Fleur nodded to a bag sitting on the steps. "Well, I was out gathering shoes. I think we can make it out this morning. I was going to wait for the water to recede, but if it's an emergency, we'd better leave sooner."

I burst into tears unexpectedly. A wall of pain and confusion pounded through me, leaving me sobbing on the stairs. Fleur's arms tentatively wrapped around me.

"You're going to be okay," she murmured in my ear. "You're going to make it."

I would, but Ighta wouldn't. It didn't make any sense.

I fought against the tears. "I can't cry yet. I have to face whatever comes next."

"You do a lot for them. It's important you take moments for yourself to feel things. You can't be everything for everyone." Fleur gave me a little more space, her hand rubbing circles on my back. "Just don't throw yourself into poisonous water next time. I might not be there to save you."

I laughed through the tears. "I'll try not to."

Fleur pressed her hard forehead against mine. "You are strong, Clyra. One of the strongest shroompeople I've ever met. I'm going to help you get Ighta out."

Ghostly tendrils crept along the floor, the ceiling, and the glass wall overlooking the city. I froze, causing Fleur to stumble into me.

What was happening?

I followed the shoots back to their source and let out a strangled cry.

Roots.

They all led back to Ighta, who'd collapsed against the glass wall, unmoving and deathly pale.

I ran, tripping over the roots, trying not to step on these precious signs of life. With nowhere else to grow, no way for them to connect with Turr, they'd stopped moving. Ighta could only sustain them for so long before the effort killed them.

I tried to pick Ighta up, their skin slick, their weight pulling them from my grasp. "Help!" I choked out, desperate.

Footsteps crossed the space behind me. The door opened and the others poured into the hall. I heard their gasps and cries, but my mind didn't register anything except Ighta's fluttering eyes.

Arms reached around me, and we pulled Ighta up off the floor. The roots dragged across the ground, tripping our steps. Some of them withered and returned to Ighta's body, but a few of the longer ones stayed, stubbornly searching for something to feed on.

If we were out in the forest, Ighta could connect with Turr and take back energy. As it was, the ground outside remained saturated in polluted water that would only harm Ighta.

"We need to get out of the city. Ighta has a chance if we can get back to the forest." I said.

Rhyse and Fleur carried Ighta back to the room and laid them on the floor. They remained unresponsive to my words.

"Clyra . . ." Leyren pulled me into a hug. "I don't think there's any coming back from this."

I pushed them away. "We're not going to give up. Come on. Fleur got shoes for us to wear. We can make it." I looked at Fleur with pleading eyes, and she silently handed out the footwear. They weren't built for our stem-like feet, and they hurt to put on, but they would protect us, and that's all that mattered.

Rhyse lifted Ighta off the ground. Roots dangled from their back, hanging over his arms. Usually a sign of strength and connection, these roots only represented death and decay.

We hurried down the stairs and into the watery world. Gross liquid rushed over our shoes. The smell hung heavy in my throat, thick and damp.

The wind attacked us. I longed for the time when the wind had been warm and enjoyable. Lately, it was only bladed.

"We need to stick together. The water is strong in

some places, and I don't want us falling over," Fleur cautioned.

We linked arms and followed behind Rhyse so we could keep an eye on Ighta. The water battled our every step. The tips of Ighta's roots hung in the water, swaying back and forth with the currents.

We pushed on in somber silence. I didn't take my eyes off Ighta. They hadn't opened their eyes, hadn't shown any signs of life other than the occasional twitch of their arm. Though Rhyse didn't complain, Ighta wasn't light, and it couldn't be easy to walk through the water carrying a limp body.

Where was Astrin? I scanned the buildings for any signs of him, but saw nothing. Fleur stayed ahead, scouting out the best route for us.

Seemingly hours of walking through broken streets passed. The journey couldn't have been that long, yet the water continued washing around us, the wind continued screaming, and Ighta didn't show any signs of getting better.

My arms grew sore, linked as they were between the others. We wavered this way and that, all of us tired and scared.

The water grew shallower as we neared the edge of the city. It washed off toward the river, following the slope of the stones. Big puddles lay scattered ahead of us.

Ighta groaned and started shivering in Rhyse's arms. We hurried forward, trying to speak to them, but they weren't fully aware, just squirming with discomfort.

"We're almost there," I assured them, hoping my words could break through their mind. I breathed silent prayers to Turr, wishing her soil could wrap around us and cocoon us until we'd healed.

Ighta's eyes opened wide as they latched onto mine. "Pl-please . . ." They could hardly form the words. "G-get me out of the city."

"We're almost out. You'll feel better once you touch the ground."

They went limp again, and I knew that wouldn't be the case. They weren't even thinking about healing anymore. They just didn't want to die surrounded by the humans' dark creations.

I turned away and focused on breathing. I wasn't the only one bearing Ighta's weight as a burden anymore, but knowing that didn't make this any easier. I glanced at the cloudy sky and screamed within the confines of my mind.

"Come on," Leyren said bravely. "Let's get Ighta home."

We picked up our pace.

The endless streets finally ran out. We rounded a building, coming face to face with Turr's wild beauty. I sobbed at the sight. I never wanted to see a human structure again.

I took one of Ighta's hands. The poison on their skin stung, but I accepted the pain. I needed to feel this moment. I matched Rhyse's pace, speaking softly to Ighta, describing the thick trees, cresting mushroom caps, and mossy ground. Each word relieved some of the tension in Ighta's body.

The pavement ended, and the soil welcomed us. I stumbled into it gratefully. Back in Turr's arms. Back in the safety of our planet.

We pressed on until the city had completely fallen out of sight. I didn't want Ighta to ever think about it again. They needed to lay on the ground, to feel Turr's life force around them.

We pushed through the underbrush until the shrubs and fungi finally closed around us, granting us privacy. There, I found a place for Rhyse to lay Ighta among the roots of a large daffodil tree.

We waited. I watched their roots, sure they would come back to life and sink into the ground. Instead, they lay limp across the mossy roots and soil.

Though Ighta spoke, I could barely hear them. I placed my ear by their lips.

"Death words," they whispered.

I looked back at the others, tears flooding my eyes. "Do any of you know the death words?" I couldn't speak them now. I barely remembered them.

Leyren stepped up. "I have some faint recollections."

"Ighta is asking for them."

Leyren knelt beside me and placed their shaking hand on Ighta's forehead. "Just as birth is the end of a previous existence and the start of something new, so is death the end of this one and the start of the next. May Ighta find their peace among the roots of

Turr, where they will lay until they are ready to grow once more."

Death words were supposed to bring peace, but these broke something in me. I wasn't just crying for Ighta anymore. I was crying for every piece of life that had been harmed by the humans.

Ighta's life force faltered beneath my fingers. Turr's pulse quickened, and the ground shook beneath us. They breathed their last, their body finally at rest among the roots.

INVIDIA

Nearly 5 Years Ago, Mere Months After the Humans First Landed

"Let me go! I can help! Please! Let me go too!" Invidia wrestled against the six arms holding them back, against the soft, dusty wings wrapped around them.

"Invidia, sweetheart, you have to stay. You cannot go with them." The moth woman's gentle words stilled something in Invidia long enough for her to drag them away from the line of wasps and bees.

"No." Tears poured down Invidia's cheeks, their eyes bloodshot from all the tears they'd shed that week. Shed for the lines of warriors who'd marched from the safety of Isagani to the human city and never returned. Shed for the frustration and helplessness they felt each time the recovery teams denied Invidia's desperate plea to help.

"It's safer for you here." With hands covered in soft, light gray fuzz, the moth woman stroked Invidia's headcap and brushed away their tears. "It's safer here for all of us."

Invidia looked up into the woman's black eyes. "But it's not. Not as long as the aliens are here. Not as long as they keep tearing Turr's bones from her body. Not as long as they keep tearing through our land and planting their parasitic crops. Lorna said we'll never be safe until they're gone."

Invidia's gaze drifted over the tops of the daffodil forest, across the valley, and to the massive metal city the humans had ripped from the land and melted together. "That's why I have to go fight. Please, Jess, let me go!"

Though Invidia screamed and struggled against her, the moth woman remained an immovable force. She beat her wings, easily dragging Invidia from the line of recruits.

"Invidia! What're you doing here?" Lorna broke away from her fellow wasps and raced over to Jess and Invidia. When Invidia saw their friend, they broke out in tears. Jess let the distraught shroomperson collapse into the wasp girl's arms.

"Shh, what're you so upset about?"

Knowing how selfish they were acting rose self-hatred in the form of bile into Invidia's mouth. It wasn't her friends and family being sent on scouting mis-sions— suicide missions— to either reason with the aliens or fight to the death trying. They were Lorna's.

But Lorna's eyes only sparkled with tears; she wasn't blubbering. Not like Invidia.

"I'm sorry, Lorna. I shouldn't be upset. You're the one who should be crying, not me."

"No, no." Lorna knelt so she could look Invidia in the eye. "Don't say that. You're entitled to whatever you're feeling, and that doesn't take away from what I feel at all. Do you understand that?"

Invidia nodded, then shook their head, because though they understood it with their mind, they weren't sure they believed it in their spirit.

"Tell me what you're feeling."

Their pink lips opened, then pouted, words jumbling up in their throat and stumbling over each other in their mind. "I want—" They couldn't continue. They shook their head, and Lorna simply rubbed their hands gently and waited.

They wanted to say they were upset to see the bees and wasps march off to battle, wanted to say they were grieving the loss, but they couldn't. Because they were upset over something much worse. They wanted to lie, but the truth forced its way from their lips instead. "I want to go with them."

For a moment, silence stretched between them. Lorna's eyes widened before she looked around. Invidia was the only shroomperson present. The others stayed in the center of the city, safe in their decomposition caves. In fact, no creature as small and delicate as a shroomperson stood nearby, only creatures who could fight and protect themselves.

"Invidia, you can't . . ." Lorna stopped when Invidia looked into her dark, shiny eyes.

"I can't what, Lorna?" They spit out the words, tripping over their tears,.

They both knew what Indivia couldn't do.

They couldn't fight. They couldn't protect. They couldn't survive.

Lorna struggled to speak the words, wrestled with the agony the truth might bring. But Invidia already drowned under the pain, even if the words remained unspoken. Though they hated Lorna for saying them, they would've hated her more for not.

"You can't fight. You can't even protect yourself." Once the first words left her mouth, the rest came out in a rush, each a shard of metal into Invidia's shredded soul. "You're not a fighter type, and even among the gentle types, you're the weakest. Shroompeople aren't meant for fighting, they're not meant for protecting. They're not even meant to be out in the storms or the sun. You can barely walk out from under the shelter of the leaves and shroomcaps. How do you think you'd be able to march through the barren lands, around the human city, and up to their walls of burning metal? Why don't you understand that?"

But it wasn't that Invidia didn't understand it. They didn't accept it. **They didn't accept being helpless, worthless, powerless.**

Invidia's hands balled into fists as tears of anger flowed down their cheeks.

"Invidia, I'm sorry." Lorna tried to pull her shroom friend into a hug, but Invidia turned away. "I shouldn't have said all that. I just—"

"You just want me to be safe."

Lorna nodded quickly, unsurely, uncertain that was the right answer.

"I know." Bitterness filled Invidia's aching chest. "Everyone wants me and all the other shroompeople to be safe. You want to save us from death, from destruction, so we can do what?" Their eyes burned into Lorna's with venom, waiting for an answer. **We'll never be safe until they're gone.**

She swallowed before croaking out, "I don't know what you—"

"What we do?" Invidia pounded their fist against their chest. "What is it that shroom Turrians do? What are we made to do?"

Lorna's face paled. "Decompose things."

"What things?" The words tasted like acid, but Invidia didn't stop them. They'd grown sick of everyone telling them what they could or could not do or what was best for them.

Lorna whispered so quietly, Invidia almost didn't hear. Almost. "Dead things."

The silence between them stretched like a million miles.

"Dead things," Invidia repeated. "So I guess you really can't save us from death, can you?"

Lorna only hung her head.

A twinge of guilt and sorrow struck Invidia. They shouldn't have made this about themself. These were Lorna's friends and family marching off to war, and Invidia wanted to throw themself at the humans right along with them, fully knowing they would die.

But wasn't it better to die trying than wait until the humans came to kill and capture them in their own caves?

"I don't want to be saved, Lorna. I want to find some sort of purpose in this new chaos. I don't want to spend my *life sifting through dead things, I want to live." With a last glance at their friend, Invidia turned and stalked back down the path to the heart of Isagani, to the shroom caves, to the acceptable death that awaited them.*

Day 7 Since Humans Made the Dead Zones

"What is my purpose?" Invidia whispered to the night. Hours had passed since the memory faded, but they'd yet to fall back to sleep. "What was I meant to do?"

But mostly they wondered if they would've even been able to make a difference, if they would've been able to make choices that could've altered the fate of their garden and friends.

But what *if* they could've? Would they be able to live with the knowledge that they could've done something different, but didn't?

A thousand scenarios rushed through their head, competing, screaming, overwhelming, each worse than the last, each driving Invidia's self-loathing deeper and deeper and deeper.

Let them go, the wind repeated over and over.

"Stop it!" Invidia sobbed, clutching their ears, struggling to block out the sound.

But it didn't just arrive on the wind. It permeated everything around them—the dirt, the air, the black water Invidia had tried consuming earlier. Even now, they felt the sludge tearing through their flesh, doing nothing but add to their overwhelming misery.

At first, they'd slept in the cave, hiding from the wind. But they couldn't anymore. Not after they'd failed to find enough food for everyone. Not after the dandelion and sunflower girls started crying because they wanted to see the sun but their bodies melted into magot food when Invidia tried to move them. Not after the little shroombabies started to scream at Invidia to decompose the snapdragon Turrians' bodies so they could eat and survive.

So despite the unyielding ground littered with metal scraps and sharp rocks, Invidia continued shivering the night away, propped up against the still, motley walls of their shroom cave. Out here, they could do nothing but listen to the wind and wonder how much more they could endure before they laid down and gave up.

"What if it's right?" A soft, muted voice from beside Invidia chased away the voice in the wind. They focused on it, trying to remember the voice as it had been before his face had crumpled away entirely.

"What if what's right, Resley?" Invidia sniffed and wiped their nose on the back of their hand, not even bothering to look at the black tears and crusty scabs clinging to their skin.

"The wind. What if . . . what if it's time for you to let us go?"

Fresh tears bubbled up in Invidia's eyes as they turned, still curled up against the wall, and tried to make out Resley's crumbling features in the foggy moonlight. "No, don't say that. I thought—" They hiccupped. "I thought you didn't want me to leave?" They would've reached out to touch his cheek if he had one left. The stench from his rotting body made them want to gag, but after three nights of sleeping next to him, they'd learned to shove it to the back of their throat along with every other thought that made them want to scream.

"Well—" He sounded like he was pushing past tears to speak. Invidia didn't know how. He didn't have eyes left to cry. "I don't. Of course I don't, but I just . . . I just don't feel good, is all."

If Invidia closed their eyes, they could almost imagine the way tears had once looked in his brilliant green eyes, so much like drops of dew on vines in the early morning. They tried to cling to that image, but darkness spread through their memory, corrupting everything it touched until only death and sorrow remained. When they looked at him again, only empty pits where his eyes had once been stared back.

"I know you don't. I know. I'm trying to figure out a way to save you."

The words felt like betrayal on their lips. Nothing was left to save. They couldn't do this on their own. They couldn't build new caves, couldn't cultivate the gardens of Isagani, couldn't purify the water, couldn't fight or protect. They were only good for decomposing, for enabling death.

But death marked the end, and they didn't want to be a part of the end anymore. They wanted a new beginning, a new life. That seemed a possibility as distant as finding a way to resculpt Resley's face from the dust and slimy globs in his lap or reattach his arm.

"Invidia?"

"Yes, Resley?" They tried desperately to hold back their tears, to be strong for him, to show some sort of hope for him to look at and feel, even if that hope had already begun to die.

"I really just want . . . a hug."

"Alright," they choked back. "You can hug me."

They couldn't hold back the sobs any longer. Wrapping their arms around themself against the cold, they waited for his arms to encircle them as well, waited for the touch of life to grace their skin once again.

The embrace never came.

Maybe I am the one who is dead.

CLYRA

Day 7 Since the Humans Left

Everything halted the moment after Ighta's death. Turr held her breath in respect for the life that moved on. Ighta now drifted within the safety of Turr's arms. I didn't quite know what that meant, but I did know they had finally found peace.

Yori sniffled. I stood and wrapped my arms around them. The others came in close, completing our mourning circle. Our sorrow mixed with relief. Ighta didn't deserve to suffer any longer.

I extracted myself from their arms and looked down at Ighta. The ground had already started to claim their body. Roots crept from the soil and wrapped themselves tenderly around the dark form. Turr showed a love for Ighta she hadn't shown to the humans. Those she had ripped apart, but Ighta she took home.

Within a few minutes, the dirt had closed over their face, sheltering them back in Turr's womb. They would fight no longer, their soul succumbing to a complete rest. I would never forget the battle Ighta fought.

Yet, I couldn't quite escape the guilt pressing in on me. Could I have done more for them? Doubt filled the space between my flesh, holding me down. Life was so unfair and we were all stuck in it, struggling to succeed when everything was stacked against us.

"We need to mark this spot. Ighta deserves that." I wanted to be able to find this place later.

While the others looked for something to serve as a memorial, I sat back down and placed a hand on the soil. Death was a weakness to those it left behind. It was a crippling disease that swept through the body and left a ruined shell. Though I still lived, this could've been any of us.

It still could be any of us.

While death had felt closer over the last few days, I'd never connected to it like I'd become now. A sharp fear harbored within me. I couldn't control death. I didn't even know what death was. How would I move on with the unknown hovering over me like that?

Rhyse returned with a large stone. In the sunlight, veins of bright red glimmered across the white surface. "I think Ighta would like this," he said, setting it down.

I helped roll it into place and imagined the future of this grove. Nature would take its course. The rocks would shift, the trees would grow, things would die and come to life, and beneath all of it would lay a memory of a time long past. This rock would remain as a permanent reminder for us, but a temporary one in the line of the past, present, and future.

Straiya stepped forward with a yellow flower, her hands cupped around the dirt and roots. She dug a hole by the stone and carefully planted it. "I think Ighta will be happy to become life again," she said softly.

I watched as grief became a place of regrowth, finally understanding what that meant.

Even in the aftermath of death, time passed. A warm breeze swept through the copse of trees, bearing the sweet smell of ripe fruit. We hadn't eaten since before the storm, and in the panic of getting Ighta out of the city, our bodies forgot their needs. Before we continued, we had to eat.

I followed the smell of fruit through the wild underbrush. The forest fell away, revealing a flattened area where neat rows of trees grew. They were young, but old enough to bear their fruit. The slender branches hung low, heavy with their own burdens.

"What is this?" Yori stepped into the strange emptiness. I'd seen this type of organization before, back in the humans' houses, where everything fit into its place.

"They can't even let plants grow naturally. They have to set them all in maddening rows." Leyren's voice dripped with disgust.

"Now that they're gone, the forest will reclaim this." I leaned down and pulled the shoes off my feet, throwing them behind me. I never wanted to wear anything like them again. The touch of grass brought relief to my soul. I followed Straiya, ignoring the commotion as the others tore off their shoes and cast them aside.

A strange quiet had settled in this unnatural grove, as if Turr's life knew to stay away. I loved peace, but not this kind of peace. This felt empty and meaningless.

Straiya jumped and pulled herself onto one of the branches. She perched, her feet balancing on the bark, and began picking fruit. "Catch!" she called, throwing them to us.

I opened my hands and caught one, the skin perfectly ripe. Sweet juices dripped over my fingers as I began to tear it apart.

Straiya gathered more and brought them down. We sat on the grass and feasted beneath the trees. I set down roots and connected with Turr. I needed her comfort now more than ever. I couldn't wait to leave this part of our journey behind. Though I couldn't see the city from here, it still loomed over us in spirit.

The others let their roots extend too. Fruit would only sustain us for so long. We needed the energy that only Turr could provide. Tapping into the human bodies had given me something similar to this energy, but it had felt strange in a way this didn't. We were fed through death, just as Turr was fed through death, but it felt better when that death came from Turr's own creatures, from her own life force.

Across the grove, Fleur settled beside Rhyse. They ate fruit and talked softly. Rhyse caught me looking and smiled. He beckoned me over, and Fleur got up to leave. I pulled my roots back into myself and crawled over.

"Are you going to be okay?" Rhyse asked.

I sat and played with the grass between us. Thinking about Ighta's death made it difficult to meet his gaze.

"Now that we're back in Turr's hands, I have a lot of hope," I said honestly. "Ighta's death, in a way, is . . . comforting. They deserved to rest. They were in too much pain."

"The city is only the beginning. Where you're headed will probably be much worse," Rhyse warned.

I didn't want to think about it, though I knew it was true. We'd be reaching the dead zones any day now. They had to be close to the city.

"We've come this far. I like to think that we're growing stronger." Only a couple days had passed since leaving the lab, and they'd been some of the hardest days of my life. But we were free, and that would keep us going.

"How would you feel if I didn't continue with you?"

My breath hitched. I wasn't surprised. I'd seen the way he acted around Fleur and Astrin. He deserved to be with them.

Still, losing two companions in one day wasn't going to be easy.

I took his hands, our palms sticking together. "You're going to stay in the city with Fleur and Astrin?"

Rhyse nodded. "They're fulfilling a role here that Turr called them to, and I want to help them with it. Others will come to the city, and they're going to need help. It just feels right to be with them." His eyes pleaded with me to understand, but I understood even before he explained.

I just didn't know how to say goodbye.

"Stay with them. It's important to you, so it's important to me. I'm grateful that I got to know you, even if it was through such horrible circumstances."

He breathed a sigh of relief. "Thank you," he said. "I was worried you'd be angry."

"Of course not. I could never be angry at you for finding your place on Turr. We'll miss you, but we'll all understand."

"It's not goodbye forever. Turr is going to heal, the dead zones are going to disappear, and we'll all meet again at some point."

I clung to those words, the promise of a better future. "Have you told anyone else?"

Rhyse shook his head. "I had to tell you first."

I lingered in those words, still holding his hands. "Thank you. That means more than you know."

He laughed. "I think I do know. We're alike, you and I, and while I hate the humans, I will never hate the fact that I met you. You're going to do amazing things."

I felt seen. I felt recognized. I felt loved.

That made it easier and harder to let him go.

We'd entered the city as six, but now left as four.

Though unexpected, the turn of events felt right. Ighta had found safety and peace, and Rhyse found others he wanted to rebuild the world with. And for those of us still heading to the dead zones, we held Turr's call deep in our chests.

We stopped at a stream to wash the sticky fruit juice away. With Turr's wild places and our roots to sustain us, we wouldn't have to eat as much. Our roots would sustain us. I scrubbed my hands and arms and splashed water across my face. It soaked into my skin, refreshing me, washing away the tears and calming my fears.

Our journey, almost over, was the beginning of Turr's healing. We felt it as an accomplishment just to be here.

I watched as Straiya, Yori, and Leyren put on brave faces. We held ourselves together for each other. One day, we would give ourselves over to grief and the healing it would bring, letting it swallow us for at least a few hours.

But today, we would keep pushing forward.

Day 7 Since Humans Made the Dead Zones

Resley's words haunted Invidia as they stepped one foot after the other, the once soft soles of their feet now calloused against the seemingly endless stretches of gravelly road.

No matter how hard they tried, they could no longer cover the death around them with greenery and life. But now, they weren't even sure they *wanted* to cover it anymore. Perhaps hiding from reality was just as difficult as facing it. No matter how horrific it seemed.

Everything was dead.

Everyone was dead.

No amount of hoping or lying to themself could change that.

They were alone.

If you take care of Turr, she will take care of you. Invidia used to live by those words. Now, they weren't sure Turr was even alive enough to care for. And if she had become so broken, how could she take care of her children again?

Turr has no use for me.

Slowly, Invidia eased to the ground, ignoring the sharp fragment of bent, scorched metal digging into their side. Tears fell down their hollow cheeks, thinner now than ever.

"I really just want a hug."

Invidia's arms circled around themself once again, but their own cold touch could never replace the warmth a hug from another living creature would bring.

The air hung still, cold, stale, silent. Invidia hadn't heard even the breath of another Turrian or plant for an untold number of days. They'd quickly lost count as the sun rose and set, alternating between scorching the barren surface of Turr below and being unable to penetrate the thick, dark fog that sometimes choked the land.

They'd been unable to accept that they truly were the last alive. But now, this new reality sunk so deep into them that even the great sobs rattling their chest weren't enough to release the pain it brought.

"Why did you leave me here? Why am I the only one left alive?" Their words hung dully on the silent air. They struggled to believe Turr could even hear them. For as far as their eyes could see, everything continued to rot, denying all life on its surface.

And what if . . . The thought tore cavities through their soul. *What if the entire planet is a dead zone? Because if it isn't, why hasn't anyone come to save me?*

The smallest whisper tickled Invidia's ear, stilling the tears for a moment.

Wiping goop from their face and sniffling, Invidia slowly pushed themself to a sitting position, ignoring how much they wanted to simply lay on the ground and wait for Turr to take them back.

The whisper came again—the same voice who'd screamed at them, commanding them to **let go**. This time, it spoke a different message.

I have not left you.

Sinking their hands into the soil, eyes blinded by tears and barely able to see the ground illuminated by the crescent moon, Invidia struggled to form words for all the things rushing through their mind, screaming for answers. "Then why? Why am I alone?"

The whisper fell silent, but a gentle, fragile breeze blew through the garden city. A couple dead leaves tossed into the air, dropping a few feet away.

Invidia blinked against the tears and stumbled to their feet. Swaying, they struggled to keep themself upright, their body feeling so, so heavy. They hadn't taken in any nutrients for days, continuing to push the starvation aside.

The breeze blew again, sending the same leaves tumbling down the path. This time, Invidia followed, one step at a time. They fell once, then twice, but each time they pulled themself back to their feet.

Turning, they glanced back, unable to see their mushroom cave from here. They didn't know where they'd end up if they followed the breeze, didn't know what awaited them if they continued. The haunting echoes of the dead creatures' screams and pleas rattled in Invidia's mind. Though they didn't want to move forward, they knew they couldn't turn back.

"Wait!" Stumbling down the road, Invidia followed as the leaves led them to a place in Isagani they'd once spent many days playing in.

Fresh tears trickled down their cheeks as they looked up to the sagging daffodil forest. Under the leaves, on the stalks, and clinging to the once strong petals hung dozens of beautifully crafted wasp nests.

"Lorna . . ." Invidia's shaking fists clenched as they bit their lip. They'd spent hours searching for their friend but hadn't been able to face coming here, to the home of the wasps who'd marched off to fight the humans in vain.

Then their eyes landed on a shock of red and green so bright against the grays, whites and blacks, it looked more like a hallucination than reality. Carried by uncertain steps, Invidia ran, collapsing next to it.

With shaking, disbelieving hands, they reached for the velvety petals, expecting them to waver and flicker away like all the other hallucinations their psychedelic properties had once created. Instead, their fingers pushed against the petals, and the flower swayed.

"I don't believe it." Invidia laughed through their tears, leaning down to smell the tantalizing, sweet scent of the blossom.

A memory flashed back, of a day they'd been playing with Lorna in the daffodil trees. Their friend had explained how the wasps built their houses. The memory tasted sweet, bringing a sweeping grin to Invidia's cracked lips.

Then the memory soured, not from the poison in the cells, but rather from their own actions and shame.

"Invidia, are you listening? I thought you wanted to learn about this." Lorna hummed brightly, but the cheeriness covered a layer of hurt.

"Huh? Oh yes, I'm listening." Invidia yawned lazily as they gently blew on the butterfly they'd let land on their hand, watching it flutter away softly.

"If you don't find this interesting, we can always go do something else." Lorna's exoskeleton reddened as she turned away.

A pang of guilt shot through Invidia as they reached out to her. "No, I want to know. I asked, and Turr knows how many times I've shown you my own home. It's only fair you show me yours."

An unsure smile spread across Lorna's face as she nodded. "If you're sure."

"I'm sure."

But though sure in their soul, Invidia's mind continued to wander. Lorna's bright eyes and happy smile as she described their sophisticated building system didn't spread to Invidia.

Tears ran down Invidia's face when Lorna finally sighed

in defeat and said, "That's okay. I know it's not interesting."

Yet as desperately as Invidia wanted to prove to their friend how much they cared about them and their life, they couldn't recall one thing Lorna had told them.

Just like they didn't remember their butterfly watching date the next week.

Invidia buried their face in their hands and cried, unable to contain the grief tearing apart their chest. "Why was I so selfish? Why couldn't I have just focused on what she was saying, just one time? Was it really so hard?"

Why did Turr save me, if I couldn't have been bothered to remember an outing with my best friend? I'm **weak, worthless, useless.**

Anger bubbled through the grief. "Why did you bring me here? Why are you reminding me of the countless ways I've failed?"

The wind swirled around the daffodil, a single petal dropping at Invidia's feet.

Pick it.

Invidia picked up the petal, obeying numbly, no longer caring what they tried since everything else had failed. They were tired. They wanted this to end. They didn't want to be the last creature alive anymore, listening to the moans of their dead friends. They wanted this pain, this regret, this grief to end.

No. Pick the flower.

Bile rose in Invidia's throat. For a moment, their fingers hovered around the stem of the flower, then collapsed. They couldn't bring themself to pluck it from the ground and end its life.

"I can't." Their head hung low. "I don't want to feast on dead things anymore. I want to enjoy life. I want to be *more* than death."

That has never been your purpose.

They jumped to their feet, screaming at the wind. "Yes it has! Look at me, Turr! Look at what you have made me to be. A shroom Turrian. What other purpose can I have? I am *destined* for death!"

The wind quieted.

For a moment, Invidia panicked, thinking Turr had abandoned them again. But before they could plead for the wind to return, the breeze caressed their face.

Pluck the flower, and I will show you.

Though anger and grief battled inside them, fighting for release, for a different way out, Invidia shoved them aside, too tired, too defeated, to let them have their way any longer.

Then the smallest seed of a feeling they'd been choking and subduing since the land had died finally sprouted.

They *wanted* to **let go**, to surrender.

"Okay," Invidia whispered through peeling lips. Bending down, they wrapped their spindly fingers around the stalk and pulled. The ripping of roots echoed in the silence. Invidia gagged.

Bury it.

Invidia shook their head, clenching their eyes

shut. They thought of the creatures back in the mushroom cave pleading for food, starving, dying.

Then Invidia remembered—they were dead already.

Hands shaking, they dug a small hole in the black, dry ground, laid the perfect, shining daffodil inside its grave, and buried it. They felt as if they'd buried all their hope with it.

Now, consume it. Release it back to me.

Invidia swallowed, their throat as gravelly as the road they'd been walking on. "I don't want to be a part of death anymore."

Then you will also forfeit being a part of life.

They wanted to fight against it, to protest against this "cycle of life" that wasn't really a cycle at all because everything ended in death. But even if they didn't eat, didn't consume the nutrients of the daffodil, they too would die, and death would still triumph.

Though the act, once as natural as sleeping, now made them gag and nauseous, they situated their feet over the grave and closed their eyes.

Nothing happened. *Has it been so long that I've forgotten how to fulfill my purpose?*

They used to experience an intimate connection with Turr. It'd been so easy to reach out, to bridge the gap between them, to feel her life. Now they felt only silence.

An empty pit opened in their soul.

None of this was real. Just as they'd hallucinated their dead friends speaking to them, so now they hallucinated Turr speaking to them. She wasn't alive. She hadn't been strong enough to fight against the humans. None of them had. Especially not Invidia.

Just as they moved to step off the grave and grieve the worthless loss of the beautiful flower, the ground shifted around their feet.

Turr was reaching out to them.

A gasp left their lips as something like love reached up through the dirt and seeped into their flesh.

Turr lived. Invidia wasn't alone.

Taking a deep breath, Invidia reached back out. A jolt of sharp pain raced up their legs as their roots broke free from the hard soles of their feet, struggling to navigate around the hard rocks and metal, but Invidia embraced the pain—a physical expression of the way their soul had felt for far too long.

The roots wrapped around the flower, hugged it, pressed against it until it became one with the dirt around it. Nutrients flowed into Invidia's body—the first they'd tasted in days.

The ever-present dizziness and lightheadedness disappeared. Their legs no longer threatened to collapse. And when they looked at their hands, they saw a flush of color rather than just the pale glow of rot.

Look, Invidia.

Hesitantly, they opened their eyes, almost scared of what they'd see.

Dots of pink scattered across the ground, spreading from Invidia's feet in a small circle.

They had to blink, wiping away a flood of tears, to convince themself it was real. They couldn't deny it, couldn't hallucinate it, couldn't ignore it. A ring of little pink and white mushrooms encircled them, connected to their roots, connected to their life force, a life force reawakened by the death of one small

flower.

If you take care of Turr ...

Let go, the wind whispered again.

This time, the words brought a hum of excitement and peace rather than horror and sorrow. Leaves danced across the ground as the breeze shifted, stronger than before as it pushed Invidia.

Let go.

She will take care of you.

Following its lead, Invidia weaved their way through the daffodil stalks, the dead flowers' presence appearing more like hope rather than hopelessness.

The leaves settled on a still body.

The light inside Invidia faded as emotion constricted their throat.

The wasp creature lay on the ground almost peacefully, though one of their once iridescent wings lay torn a few feet away.

Invidia took a step back, shaking their head. The wind pushed against them. "I don't . . . I can't . . ." They wanted to believe this was a random wasp who'd died when the humans left Turr, but something deep inside them knew they weren't.

Licking their lips. Invidia stepped forward, trying to trust Turr, trying to trust the force who'd once taken care of them in such perfect balance before the humans. Grappling their anxiety, they placed a hand on the creature's shoulder and rolled them over.

A cry tore from their lips as they fell back, scrambling away from the soft, half-missing face staring dully at the dead flowers above.

Let her go.

But Invidia couldn't. As much as they tried, they couldn't **let go** of all the times they'd been so selfish, all the times they'd forgotten a special date, all the times they'd proven over and over how bad of a friend they were. Yet despite all those failures, Lorna had never given up on Invidia, had never **let them go.**

So how could Invidia? How could they let her go, bury her deep in the ground and then decompose her body until nothing remained to remember?

They'd done nothing but take and take and take from their community, their friends, from Turr. Were they really going to stand over Lorna's body and do nothing but take once again?

"Lorna, I'm so sorry." Invidia crawled back to her half-rotted body. Taking her light head into their arms, they cradled her, rocking her back and forth. "I'm so sorry, Lorna, for not caring more, for not listening more or remembering more. I never did anything for you, and yet you always made me feel so special. I don't know why you were my friend or why you loved me so much. I didn't deserve a friend like you." Invidia pressed their forehead to Lorna's, gagging when some of her skin and exoskeleton crumbled away. "I can't let you go."

They gazed into their friend's glazed eyes. "Why won't you say something? Please, say something. Let me know you forgive me. I can't go on thinking you don't know how much I care, how much you meant to me. Please."

But unlike all the other dead creatures, Lorna's face remained still and her voice stayed quiet in her mouth—silent, like death always should be.

All creatures have their faults, the wind whispered, but Invidia barely paid it attention. The numbness in their heart overwhelmed all else.

You are not the only creature who lived with regrets.

Invidia turned their angry eyes to the wind. "Maybe, but were any of them as rebellious and problematic as me? I don't remember any of them revolting against the very order of life, against their purpose. I spent more time wishing I were something, *someone*, else, rather than appreciating what I was made for. I rebelled against the balance and the perfection of the garden, of the very order *you* set into place. Did anyone else have such unforgivable faults as those?"

I did not make a mistake with you.

Invidia shook their head. "How could you not have?"

I saved you for a reason.

"To punish me? So I could be reminded of my misgivings, failures, regrets? So I could see all my friends like—" They couldn't finish the words as they glanced down at their once beautiful and vibrant friend, now still and dull in death.

The humans disrupted the balance. Sorrow hummed through the ground and sparked through the atmosphere. "I don't think . . . I don't think anything will ever be the same."

The planet was dying.

Bitterness swallowed Invidia. Even Turr couldn't fix this damage.

But maybe I don't want it to be the same. The words came so quiet, Invidia wasn't sure they heard them right. **That's why I saved you. Balance the way it existed before the humans can no longer continue. New balance must be made. That is why I chose you. You, a little psychedelic shroom born with hopes and**

dreams beyond the compost pile, had the ability to en-vision things differently, including life and death it-self. You are the only creature who can understand.

Invidia clenched their jaw. "But I *don't* under-stand."

You will, if you let go. If you let her go.

Everything inside Invidia balked as they looked down at their friend, at the little black beetle crawl-ing out of her ear and back in through her nose. They tried to remember her as she'd once been: bright red exoskeleton, eyes shimmering black, wings catching the light and scattering it into rainbows.

When they opened their eyes, they knew deep down, Lorna didn't want to remain like this, to be remembered like this. No matter what regrets In-vidia held over their friendship, Lorna had loved them anyway. Because of that, she must've somehow known just how much Invidia loved her too.

Turr was right.

They had to **let go**.

Placing Lorna's body down, Invidia grabbed a small scoop-like rock, the familiarity of their pur-pose flooding back to them.

Each time they struck the rock against the un-yielding dirt, they poured out their regrets and **let them go.**

"I'm sorry I couldn't protect you. I'm sorry I couldn't protect any of us: Indigo, my shroomparent, the wasps and bees that went to war, Lowen, Resley, my shroombabies."

The hole grew in size.

"I'm sorry I couldn't find a way to exist in harmony with Isagani. I'm sorry I couldn't conform to what was expected of me."

The hole was almost big enough.

"I'm sorry I didn't **let go** earlier."

With tender hands, they rolled Lorna into the grave, the air ringing with a hollow thud. Invidia took one last look at their friend, then closed their eyes. As they moved dirt over her body, they remembered her the way she'd been in life.

Then they stood over the grave. The roots grew easily and painlessly from the bottoms of their feet, wrapping around Lorna's body in one last hug before letting go.

The ground quaked, and the wind swirled voraciously. Then all fell silent as a single, gentle sigh moved from the land.

Thank you.

Invidia's body filled with life and strength. When they looked down, black veins no longer riddled their skin, their flesh no longer tethered together by hope alone. Dozens of little mushrooms sprang up around them, filling the once bleak landscape with spots of pink and white. Though they still felt the damage within their cells, still found pockets of death clinging to their skin, they existed in harmony with it now. No longer did it drag them to unimaginable depths.

Tears rushed down Invidia's cheeks as they turned

to the daffodil tree beside them. Bright green life spread from the bottom of its stalk, racing faster and faster up its length, filling the leaves with vibrant life and strength. The life force reached the top of the flower and its wilted petals bloomed bright yellow with life.

A warmth like they hadn't felt in countless days spread through them. Invidia stumbled to the flower tree, brushing away tears that hung to the back of their hand—clear, no longer black.

"Oh, Lorna." They wrapped their arms as far around the daffodil tree's stalk as they could reach. As they closed their eyes, feeling the life pulsing through the flower, they imagined Lorna reaching out with all six of her legs and enveloping them in a strong hug.

They understood now. Their purpose had never been about death. It had only ever been the beginning of new life.

CLYRA

Day 7 Since the Humans Left

A small ship hung in the trees. It rocked gently, held up by thick vines.

We stepped cautiously into the clearing. Glass glittered in the grass. The forest beyond the city was unlike the one outside the lab. A battle had taken place here when Turr, in her justified rage, tore ships apart to gain her freedom. Shrapnel lay scattered across the underbrush. Gouges from the ships cut across the ground.

Straiya ran under the ship, craning her neck to take it in. Before we could stop her, she jumped, grabbed onto its underside, and clambered up. Though her weightlessness had begun to return, I didn't like seeing her up there, unsure if the ship would hold. I bit my tongue.

"What do you see?" Leyren asked.

Straiya leaned over the top and peered in. "There are bodies. Three of them." She reared back, face scrunched in disgust. "They're not rotting very fast."

"Makes sense. Turr can't reach them properly," Leyren said.

"I'm coming up." I ran to one of the trees holding up the ship and started climbing. The branches, all within reach of each other and thick enough to hold my weight, made the trek easy. The strain of the climb brought a grin to my face even as my muscles strained and burned.

I didn't just want to see the ship. I'd seen more than enough wreckage and bodies. I wanted to climb up higher where I could see everything. Maybe I'd even get my first glimpse of the dead zone.

My fingers searched the rough bark for handholds. My feet slipped into the crevices between the branches. A thin layer of sweat beaded on my skin. I reached the midway point where the branches bowed beneath the weight of the ship. Straiya waited for me, leaning against the trunk. She took my hand and pulled me up, helping me keep my balance.

Leyren and Yori watched as Straiya led me out to the aircraft. Balancing on the vines wasn't easy. I looked down and caught Leyren shaking their head in amusement. I refocused all my energy to not slip and fall. Straiya continued pulling me forward as I fought the panic burning in my stomach. I wasn't as nimble as her and had to take smaller steps.

The ship swayed beneath us. I crouched down, letting go of Straiya, and crawled on my hands and knees until I could see through the glass. The bodies were at a gross stage of decay. Skin slid off the bones, stretching so thin I could see right through it. I looked at their faces, eyes long gone and mouths open in one last act of a terrified scream. I hoped they'd felt nothing but fear and pain just before death—a mere taste of the suffering they'd forced upon us.

Bugs swarmed the corpses, exuding a smell of visceral decomposition. The bodies almost came to life beneath their touch, writhing, squirming, trying to escape even after death. Little groves of mush-rooms pushed through the graying rot of arms and legs, leaving gaping holes in the slipping skin. Small ferns curled around bones, roots traveling through emptying veins.

What the humans deserved in life, they'd received in death.

"It's almost beautiful," Straiya breathed. I looked at her and she turned red. "I mean it's gross, but it also feels . . . right."

I laughed. "I was thinking the same thing. This is what they deserve." A shiver of glee ran through me. I stood back to allow fresh air to enter my system. The scent of death, strong and overwhelming, made me dizzy with life.

The heavy wind through the canopy shifted where we stood. I spread my arms and let the air wrap itself around me. I wasn't scared of this height any-more. How could I be when Turr filled all the space around us?

"We should go higher. I want to look for the dead zone." I grabbed Straiya, wanting her support as we crossed over the vines.

We made it back to the tree and started to climb. I grew shakier as we reached higher, my fingers tight-ening around the shrinking branches. Straiya's words of caution were lost in the wind.

Just when I thought I couldn't go any higher, my head poked through the branches and I got a view of everything around us. I looked back to where the city's remains tried to scrape the heavens. The forest we'd walked through grew thick and healthy, aside from some places where ships had crashed, but on the other side of us the forest began to thin.

And beyond it all lay the dead zone.

I gasped. Straiya grabbed onto me, her hands shaking.

A clear line ran between the forest and the dead zone. The dead zone stood like a skeleton slowly losing its bones. What had once been alive now lay completely obliterated, a wasteland of bleak darkness. I'd been expecting death, but not to this degree.

I shuddered. I couldn't bear to see Turr in this state.

"How are we supposed to fix this?" Tears streamed down my face. I'd never felt so hopeless. My chest felt like a gaping cavity filling with water. I drowned beneath the weight of my words.

Straiya leaned forward, awkwardly trying to hug me without pushing us both out of the tree. "I wish I had an answer. I really do."

We'd known this wasn't going to be an easy task. But I saw nothing to even build from. We'd just learned about death making way for new life . . . but this death was nothing like that.

How could the humans do something as evil as this? This extended even farther than the city and lab. Their blatant disrespect for life made their hunt for a new home obvious. If they'd done this to their own home planet, I knew for sure it must've rejected them. Instead of dying out, removing their stain from their planet, they'd simply spread their disease of greed to the darkness between stars.

I slumped against Straiya. "I don't think I can do this," I whispered.

"Don't say that. We're doing this together." Straiya reassured me.

The visions had been incomprehensible, but they hadn't fully prepared me for the horror waiting for us. The black death seeping across the ground reached out to drag me in, drowning all hope.

"I want to go down." I pulled myself from Straiya's grasp and started making my way back through the branches. The panic made my body feel so small. I couldn't find words to describe the incredible depth of sorrow trapped within me. No tears could drain me dry.

Darkness staked its claim. I explained to Yori and Leyren what I'd seen and watched them draw up conclusions in their minds. We weren't ready for this. The last few days had left us raw, and we couldn't push ourselves into another place of death.

I collapsed against a mushroom and slid to the ground. Turr cut through the hopelessness with a gentle insect song—a breath of song, but not enough. It sounded like a future I wasn't sure we'd see.

No kind of future awaited us in the face of such

inescapable death.

The hanging ship shrieked in the sudden brisk wind. The sound cut through my thoughts, bringing me back to life.

"Are you really giving up?" Straiya asked, sitting beside me.

"Don't you want to give up?"

Straiya didn't respond. Yori and Leyren looked away. Their silence spoke volumes.

"I'm tired of this. Every time we push past an obstacle, we have to face something even bigger. I want us to find a safe space to just exist. Why are we always *fighting* something?" I leaned my head back and looked at the sky peeking through the trees.

"You've been pushing us along this entire time. You kept telling Ighta to believe. Now that you see the dead zone, you're done? This has been our destination all along," Leyren said bitterly.

I jumped up, anger burning beneath my skin. "Climb up there and look at it yourself. Tell me how you feel after you've seen the face of death."

"We're not on our own. We—"

"Not alone? We've been nothing but alone since we started this journey. Turr keeps telling us there's more shroompeople, and I've seen them in my visions, but where are they? Maybe we're the only ones trying to make a difference. Maybe we need to follow the others' example and accept that Turr can't handle this. That we're doomed."

"You don't believe that," Yori whispered from

where they sat. They clutched their arm. "You saw Turr heal me."

I looked at the three of them, horror and pain written across their faces. Ighta's death had chipped cracks in our resolve, and now I'd finished its destruction. I'd worked so hard to hold everyone together. Now I couldn't even find the scattered pieces of myself to hold once again.

I turned my back on them. "Don't follow me," I said, running into the dark. I ignored their yells, begging for me to come back.

I had to get away. Fear devoured me from the inside out. I couldn't be the one who always believed. It had worn me down, peeled back my strength. Finally, my naive confidence had crushed me. Just like Ighta said it would. Would they like to know that they'd been right?

Tears dripped down my face. I could hardly see, the world drowning in night. I couldn't even call on my own light. All warmth seeped out of me.

Seeing the dead zone reminded me of Ighta sinking into the ground. I couldn't stop thinking about the way they'd accepted death in the end, taking it as the natural next step. I wasn't ready for that step yet.

When I felt I'd put enough space between me and the others, I settled in the crook of a large root, letting it act as walls around me. I almost missed the comfort of the lab. After the humans left, it'd become a sort of home. We'd turned it into a safe space. I yearned for its confines because right now, the world had become too big for me to control, and that frightened me more than a cage ever could.

Day 8 Since the Humans Left

My skin burned from the rough bark's bite. I moved, half asleep, trying to escape the uncomfortable sensation. It followed my motions. I pulled on the light within me, barely able to muster up a weak glow. The blue struggled to travel across my **torn skin. I screamed as the light reflected off the glossy bodies of beetles eating away at my flesh. They gathered on my arms, their small mandibles digging faster than I thought possible. I felt no pain. Only numb panic.**

I swatted at them, but they'd already burrowed into my skin, entering the home within my body. I picked them off. The detachment I felt from my body horrified me. It made me want to feel pain, if only to know I still lived. The bugs scurried through me, racing along my veins. I opened my mouth, but couldn't muster a scream past whatever lodged in my throat.

The prickling legs ran up my spine. I threw myself against the tree, rolling to crush them. They hungered for my mind. Time was running out. If they chewed away at my very being, I'd no longer be able to fight them.

I felt them in my neck.

I felt them in my cheeks.

I felt them behind my eyes.

Then I felt nothing.

Nothing remained when all I was got taken away.

I lay, the hum of my life force slowing, the rushing of my cells turning to a trickle. The world lost all its meaning.

A strange tingling broke through. I was too aware of the prison of my body. Then the weight of existence lifted off me, and I died.

I lurched, my body seizing. I couldn't breathe. The air hung so heavy it crushed me. I scrambled away from the tree, almost surprised to not feel my skin peeling away with it.

"*Clyra,*" the wind whispered.

I tried to scream, but couldn't.

"*You who spoke of belief, yet who finds yourself drowning in doubt.*"

I dug my fingers into the dirt. I was not alone out here.

"*Continue on your way. When you reach the end of this journey, you'll see that the end is where it truly begins.*"

Turr?

"*You once said all one had to do to hear me was open their heart. Your heart has been open and unguarded this entire time. Even when you don't, you still want to believe.*"

I stopped moving. All tiredness drained from my body, leaving behind a soul buzzing within its confines. Could I leave my body behind to join this free being filling the air around me?

"One day you will join me here, as your friend did, but only if I survive. I need you, Clyra. I need all of you. Come as you are and together, we can save ourselves."

I gave in to the peace filling me, my body shaking, tears flowing, finally feeling okay with accepting who I was. I'd spent so long doing what was right for others, I'd forgotten how comforting it felt to hear someone speak of my own needs.

"I have noticed your sacrifices. You are not alone. You are not responsible for everyone."

Turr telling me I wasn't responsible for everyone set me free. I lay on my back, and my roots emerged. For the first time since I'd left the lab, they searched for more than energy. This time, they yearned to connect with Turr's very core.

Time passed strangely. When I felt able, I pulled my roots back. I had to return to the others. Light had begun seeping into the sky, and I knew they'd wake soon, wondering if I'd return.

I ran, my fear replaced with hope. I shook with excitement when I burst back into the clearing.

They slept beneath the ship. Yori and Straiya had curled together, chasing away the chill with their nearness. One of the trees swayed, and I looked up to find Leyren climbing down. They stepped, slow and careful, mouth tight with concentration. Their eyes met mine and a tentative smile crossed their face. I waited for them at the bottom.

"I had to see the dead zone."

"I know," I said softly.

"It's bad, but there's something there. Something you missed. A spot of color. Maybe a piece of life." Their face shone bright with hope.

"I know." I took their hands and held them close. "I spoke to Turr. We're doing this. All of us."

We waited for the others to wake. This part of our journey would end today. Relief flourished in the realization that we would meet one of our goals. I tried not to dwell on the fear straining to build beneath my skin.

"I'm scared," I confessed.

Leyren took my hand. "I'd be concerned if you weren't. Change is always frightening."

"Yet it's necessary." I closed my eyes and leaned against the tree. If I focused, I *felt* Turr beneath me. When she'd spoken to me, I'd regained something of the connection I'd thought I was losing. Now I knew for certain she stood with us here. I didn't need to fear.

"For what it's worth, you've been very brave on this journey. Every time I wanted to give up, you were there pushing us forward. I have a lot of respect for you."

Leyren's words touched my soul. I couldn't stop the smile spreading across my face. It faltered as I remembered the way I'd run away from the only ones I could rely on. "I gave up last night."

"You didn't give up. You got overwhelmed. There's a big difference. If you'd given up, you wouldn't be here right now."

The ship creaked, Yori turned, and the day shifted into something normal. I watched Yori and Straiya begin to wake up.

"Thank you, Leyren." I hugged them.

Turr hummed beneath us.

INVIDIA

Day 8 Since Humans Made the Dead Zones

Slow, soft footsteps carried Invidia away from the daffodil forest and wasp nests back to their little makeshift mushroom cave.

They paused, the darkness of the night beginning to shift into the hazy light of morning. Weak rays of light scattered through the damaged fungus trees and danced on the ground, the walls of the broken caves, and Resley's face.

Tears collected in Invidia's eyes, but they quickly brushed them away, taking step after step until they stood over his disintegrating body, finally seeing him for what he truly was—dead.

"Resley?" Their whisper came so quiet it almost drifted away on the gentle breeze circling them, encouraging them to move forward and **let go.**

For a long moment, nothing moved—not Resley, not even the black leaves on the ground as the wind shifted over them. Then something like the sound of a breath entering lungs filled the air, and Resley's voice moved from the hollow space where his head used to be.

"Invidia, you came back."

They could only nod, though they knew he couldn't see.

Kneeling before him, they reached out to take his hand, then hesitated, their fingers hovering just over his exposed stalks and dried leafy flesh. "Resley, I—" They swallowed. "I found Lorna."

They thought they heard him smile.

"Is she alright?"

A moment passed, then another as Invidia struggled to find the words to say. Lorna wasn't "alright", she was dead; just like they all were. But . . . that didn't mean she wasn't alright. Invidia thought of the daffodil tree: alive, vibrant, strong, beautiful. A place Lorna would've found perfect for her own nest. That daffodil grew on because of Lorna, because of Turr's beautiful circle of life. No one ever truly died, they simply moved on to exist in a new and beautiful way.

"Yes." Invidia finally nodded, a small smile cracking their lips. "She's doing just fine."

"Is it beautiful?"

Invidia looked up, wishing they could see his face just once more, could see the way his eyes had shone blue against the green of his skin and vines of his hair. "What?"

"The tree."

Invidia's heart lurched in their chest.

"How . . . how did you know?"

He laughed—a sound they hadn't heard for days, weeks maybe. Hearing it   brought tears of joy to their eyes. "I heard Turr speaking to you while you were gone. I heard what she said, about life. About the way things never really die. I felt the life of something move into you and bring you back to life. I know Turr is responsible for all of this, for the balance of life. And I think . . . I think she saved you with a piece of . . . me."

Invidia collapsed to the ground, a wave of memories crashing over them.

"It's alright," Resley murmured as darkness filled the land. The moss beneath their feet began to turn black. The poison crept into their toes.

"I'm scared." Invidia wrapped their arms around Resley's neck, trying to ignore the blackness seeping through the veins of the vines growing from his body, encasing them in leafy protection.

But his protection wasn't enough. None of their efforts had been enough to protect themselves against the humans.

Tears filled Resley's eyes as the blackness raced up his neck, darkening the blue in his gaze. "Don't be." He tried to smile, a single leaf brushing Invidia's shallow cheek. "Turr will take care of you."

The pain entering Invidia's body with the black poison drew screams from them they didn't know they were capable of.

Invidia and Resley collapsed to the ground together as everything around them grew dark, dry, and dead. The darkness didn't diminish when Invidia opened their eyes; it consumed, overwhelmed, becoming impossible to escape.

The screams in the distance faded. The breath in their cells dissipated.

Death hovered over them. They felt it the same way they felt it in the compost, only this time, it grew inside them.

But as they closed their eyes to succumb to the pain and darkness, a breeze brushed across their face. The hum of life crept into their body as Resley's arms fell heavy and still around them.

Uncertain roots from their feet wrapped around Resley's ankles, encouraged by the breeze to take a little bit of his fading life force to keep their own ablaze.

Then darkness filled everything.

Invidia rocked back and forth, unable to stop the memory from washing over them. Resley had saved them from the poison just long enough for Turr to transfer a piece of his life into them. In a way, he'd never really died.

The sun peeked over the horizon. Morning loomed inevitable, just like Invidia's need to let Resley go. Finally, words returned to them as the echoes of the memory faded away.

"I was so worried about leaving you, but actually, you're the one who never left." They closed their eyes, feeling him nod.

He wasn't alive in the body in front of them; he hadn't been for a long time. Just like Lorna, he lived on in Invidia, in the wind, in Turr, and it was time for them to **let him go.**

The sensation of warm arms encircled Invidia as small tears trailed down their cheeks.

"I'm ready to go. I *want* to go," he whispered. "I'm ready to . . . rest."

Invidia nodded, feeling his hug for a few more long moments before they willed their body to move, to fulfill their purpose and Resley's.

"Don't be scared, Invidia." Resley sighed as they dug a shallow grave for his body and covered him in Turr's final embrace. "I'll always be with you. We all will."

Any words Invidia wanted to say stopped in their throat as they extended their roots into the ground and released his life back into Turr.

When they opened their eyes, they couldn't help but laugh through their tears. Their little mushroom cave had become encased by Resley's heart-shaped vines. The plants formed a strong wall between the surface of Turr and the sky surrounding her. Though not the mud walls Invidia was used to, they thought it perfect and beautiful, but best of all, they knew it was *alive*.

Turr was right.

The balance of life couldn't go back to the way it had been before the humans. But for the first time since the aliens landed five years ago, Invidia didn't want it to go back.

When they pushed back the doorway of vines and stepped into the green cave, they finally faced the creatures whose bodies they'd collected and hallucinated life into. No longer did the dead reach with decaying hands. No longer did they scream and beg out of beetle-filled mouths. They simply lay there quietly, waiting to be released back to Turr.

With renewed life and purpose flowing through their spirit, Invidia dug individual holes for each of the bodies and, one by one, gave them back to Turr. The moss and ferns outside their mushroom cave sprouted green and vibrant. Resley's vines stretched into the next mushroom cave, readying it for the day when mushrooms would fill it the same way they now filled Invidia's cave, spilling out into the once barren garden city.

Soon, only the shroombabies remained.

Invidia's heart ached as they gathered the tiny bodies to them, cradling them in their arms. Though they knew Turr would take their life back and let them live in another way, Invidia took the time to mourn that these babies would never grow to be shroompeople, that they would never be able to teach them their beautiful purpose or watch them grow and find companionship in each other.

That they would never truly call Invidia their dama.

As they placed the little bodies together into a sor-rowfully small grave, Invidia felt they were burying the last chance they had of companionship. Though they didn't want to hallucinate their life anymore, though they knew it was disrespectful to the dead to hoard their bodies and withhold them from Turr, the crushing loneliness almost made Invidia dig them back up.

But they didn't.

The air moved quietly, now clean, fresh, *alive*. Each breath Invidia took came easier than the last. Though their soul still ached with loss, it didn't consume them anymore, leaving space for a shimmer of hope.

Yes, they were alone. Though they could feel Resley's life inside of them, it now lay silent, his voice gone with his body. They still didn't know how far the dead zones stretched or how they would manage to bring life back to it all. But they were learning that it wasn't their responsibility to worry about the whole world, only the things they'd been given to nourish and cultivate.

That still didn't stop them wondering and wishing.

They stepped out of their cave, trying not to cry when they looked at the life springing forth around them, moving inch by inch as new mushrooms decomposed the dead matter, bringing life back to the city. Already an entire fungus tree stood plump and shining once again, the holes in its headcap healing slowly. Shade from its massive reach landed perfectly on the two new mushroom caves.

Invidia's heart swelled. The second mushroom cave felt like a promise somehow. Though they didn't want to get their hopes up, they couldn't help but smile, thinking that some shroomperson out there might one day make their way to Invidia and this little home that awaited them.

"If you take care of Turr, she will take care of you." This time, as Invidia whispered the old saying, they truly believed it.

Turr was alive. The planet was alive. And she was caring for her children once again.

Moving through the garden city, Invidia worked tirelessly, finding bodies, digging graves, giving back to Turr, and watching the circle of life move around them, bringing color and vibrancy back to the once desolate land.

When the noon sun shone high above them, they collapsed under a large fungus sapling to watch it grow. Pride and a sense of accomplishment grew in their chest.

They'd found their purpose at last.

"I want to share this with someone. I want to help someone else find their purpose."

As if in answer, the breeze moved past, pulling their attention to one of the nearby hills protecting the valley like it always had.

Invidia frowned, scrambling to their feet. Squinting against the sunlight, they strained to see what moved on the top of the hill.

It looked like color and life.

Like Turrians.

Invidia shook with anticipation. "It's probably just a hallucination," they tried to assure themself, to calm their fragile hope.

But when Turr whispered into their ear, they abandoned the small compost bucket they'd been filling, dirt spilling onto the ground as they left it far behind.

Laughing, they waved their arms,

shouting at the creatures, trying to be seen and heard, trying to welcome them into the city, to welcome them *home*.

Move forward, the wind whispered once more.

CLYRA

Day 8 Since the Humans Left

The border of the dead zone cut deep into Turr's skin. The ground grew tough beneath our feet. Dead plants gave way to vulnerable, bare, damaged planet skin.

Turr grew quiet when we reached the edge. I'd just started noticing her presence, but now she felt like an echo. We weren't a strong enough tether for her. Not yet.

The nightmarish scape stretched forever. I couldn't ignore the flickering memories invading my mind. Though many of my memories hadn't survived the lab, I couldn't ignore the familiarity of this place. This used to be a city built from Turr's bones. It thrived off the life she gave, all of it growing in harmony. I remembered the structures made from plant growth. I remembered the way Turr had always been present.

Now it lay as a patch of rotting flesh. A nauseating smell clung to the air—the stench of humans and their slick oils and chemicals.

"Look at that." Leyren directed us to a speckle of growing life, so small the destruction nearly swallowed it whole. A fungus tree expanded from the ground, the colors of life flowing through its soft flesh. From underneath it, a shroomperson, so dark they blended into the deathly colors around them, ran toward us, waving their arms as if scared we wouldn't notice them.

They were the shroomperson from my visions. As they drew closer, I noticed the ways they'd changed. Instead of sagging under death's weight, they moved in tune with it, its presence growing on them like a second skin. I sensed the heavy connection between us. The sort of connection only built through shared pain.

I forced myself forward. Taking my first step into the dead zone overwhelmed me with terror. All at once, the ground became serrated. Shards of stone and shrapnel from the ships littered the soil. I winced as they dug into my soles. I couldn't blame Turr for avoiding this place; if it were my skin, I'd avoid it too. I ignored the physical pain. It was nothing compared to the mental turmoil washing around inside me. I needed to hold onto the shroomperson and feel them in my hands. I needed to connect physically and assure them, and myself, that we'd all come together to heal.

The distance closed between us.

We scrambled into each other's arms, stumbling

and falling, the ground biting into our soft skin. Rubbery, broken flesh and tears, pain and sorrow, and in the middle of it, soft hands on my shoulders and something akin to comfort easing through me.

The world changed. It grew brighter and more colorful. I gasped, tears flowing from my eyes. I hadn't felt so whole in all my life. It was as if a broken piece of me had just been reconnected. Simply being here, holding this shroomperson, feeling the fragments of their pain that fit perfectly beside mine . . . it was all too much.

Their warm tears mixed with mine. We had no need for words or names at a time like this.

We'd connected much deeper than that.

We'd connected through our souls.

We trailed behind Invidia. Quiet silence, one that almost felt alive, hummed between us as they led us through the dead zone. This was their home more than it was ours. As we stepped through twisted ruins and across broken paths, I couldn't imagine the deep-rooted hurt they must feel seeing their home in this state. Maybe the things I saw as strength—their stiff posture and careful words—were actually walls, holding themself together.

We followed their lead blindly. After the initial introductions, they said they had a place to show us. We passed by the fungus tree. Scattered around it lay freshly covered mounds.

Graves.

Was Invidia the only one left alive? Had they buried all the dead they'd found? The pain of putting everyone they knew to rest must've been absolutely suffocating.

Could I do this?

You can.

I didn't feel ready.

You are.

I shuddered. Death pressed in from all directions. No life was meant to handle this much destruction. Everything that made us *us* had been torn away. Stripped of our homes, our people, and our planet, we were forced to figure out who we were when all we knew faded away.

I didn't know who I was. Now that I stood in the remains of my home, I realized just how lost I'd become. Echoes of familiarity weren't enough to re-place the core of myself I'd lost.

I looked back at the forest. As Invidia kept walk-ing forward, I wanted so badly to turn and flee to the life out there. Simply avoiding the human scars seemed so much easier.

Yori took my hand. "Come on. You're not facing this alone."

Invidia turned. "We're here." Behind them rose strange formations—a little community of makeshift caves. "When I'd finally given in and trusted Turr, finding a way to bring life back to her, she made me a new home. She must've known you were coming." Tears sparkling in their eyes. "She started making yours too."

Homes. What a strange concept in a wasteland like this. Terrifying, yet somewhat comforting.

"Why didn't you leave the dead zone? Why stay here after almost dying?" I asked.

They faltered, stalling their answer by stooping to pick up a broken mushroom cap. "At first, I didn't . . ." Tears sparkled in their eyes but they continued. "I didn't know what happened. I'd woken up to a world where everything was dead and black. I couldn't comprehend it, couldn't begin to accept that everything I knew, everything and everyone I loved, had just . . . ceased to exist. I did the only thing I knew how—I lied. I covered the death with a hallucination and forced myself to keep fighting for that lie, as if that would make it real."

Shaking their head, they took a deep breath, putting the past behind them. "But after I stopped lying to myself, after I finally faced the destruction, I stayed because this is the only home I've ever known, and this is where Turr wanted me. I've no reason to leave it behind. This is where my purpose is. Once I accepted who I am, who Turr made me to be, I realized all this death is just another beginning, not an end. Turr has been teaching me how to heal her. The garden city isn't gone forever, just waiting to be found again."

I sniffled. Invidia had gone through so much, and

they'd done it on their own. I wanted to pick them up, hold them close, and let them know they'd never be alone again.

"I have something else to show you." Invidia's face grew solemn and dark. "Something I need help with. It's not going to be easy or pleasant, but it's what Turr needs us to do."

Invidia led us to death. The sickly smell filled the air before we saw the first body—a shroomperson. They lay broken beyond recognition. The dead zone could not receive the dead. Turr was unable to open the ground to accept them.

I covered my mouth, eyes stinging. To see our fellow Turrians in death like this was harder than anything I'd come across so far. Even Ighta's death had been easier to bear. At least they'd been buried immediately.

"Turr is crying out to receive the dead. Right now, their lives can't properly return to her because of the humans' toxins. We need to release them to her." Invidia knelt, their hands briefly touching the rotting skin of the shroomperson. Their shoulders slouched, and I wondered if they knew this shroomperson.

It hit me then, the full weight of the horrors Invidia had faced. Every body was connected to them in some way, from either a close relationship or vague recognition.

"For a long time, I held onto them. I didn't want them to leave me, but—" Invidia broke off mid-sentence.

I knelt beside them, and the others followed my lead. "Just tell us what we have to do."

Invidia started digging, their small hands clawing through the tough ground, overturning it. The dirt clung to their fingers, black as night. Once, the color had meant fertility. But this ground held nothing lifelike in it. Not yet, at least.

We shaped the hole into a shallow grave for the shroomperson. Then, we carefully lifted them and placed them into its waiting mouth.

Leyren cried, mouth open, tears streaming, silent sobs wracking their horrified body. I wrapped an arm around their shoulder, my hand leaving smudges of dirt on their skin. "Are you going to be okay?"

They leaned closer, their head resting against my shoulder. "I don't know."

The overwhelmingly potent mixture of grief and hope in the air overturned my emotions.

Gently, we filled the grave with dirt. Once I could no longer see the body, I breathed easier. Looking death in the face was hard. Especially when it was an ugly, vulnerable death.

"Let's join hands." Invidia reached for the others. "I need all the shroompeople to *feel* what I'm doing, not just see."

I joined hands with Invidia and Leyren. Invidia's eyes closed. I waited, then shivered as something rushed through me. Our roots extended into the ground, a glorious feeling. The very core of who I was dug into the ground, reaching out to touch the inner being of Turr.

I threw my head back, eyes closed, overcome with the idea of becoming one with the planet again. A smile crossed my face. We stood on a grave that meant so much more than death.

Then I felt the life below us shift. Intimately, I became aware as the body seeped into the dirt around it, giving in to Invidia's gentle encouragement to let go, to become something *more*. Following Invidia's lead, I added my own encouragement and comfort.

When we opened our eyes, the grave had been transformed. Plants of all kinds bloomed, thicker ones rising between us to touch the sky. Daffodil and fungus trees took their former positions of glory.

Straiya jumped, her body taking flight midair, and stood on the top of the fungus tree. She looked to the sky and let loose a wild cry. It echoed over all of Turr, an all-consuming call that drew us all in.

I tightened my grip on the hands I held. This might not be the end we'd hoped for. So many more of the dead awaited rest, but with each burial we facilitated, we took back more and more of what was ours.

Finally, I began to understand what it was to heal. Instead of happening all at once, like I'd expected, healing was a long hard process, sometimes seeming to take more than it gave.

But each breakthrough brought us closer to who we once were. Each breakthrough closed the scars on our planet's skin just a little more. And in turn, our own scars began to close as well.

That was healing.

TURR

Day 301 Since Turr Reclaimed Her Skin

It took time, but a day came when Turr woke to the sun shining, the sky clear and quiet, and the land still and solid.

She took a deep breath, then let it out slowly. It'd been years since she'd felt like this. Peace rested on her skin and love in her bones. Turning her focus, she shifted her life force to the regrowing city of Isagani.

Plants made their way up mismatched trellises, cultivated in messy rows. Little houses, huts, and nests dotted the land and daffodil trees. Bees, wasps, and butterflies flittered between the flowers and the ground, some of them pollinating, others helping collect compost. Shroompeople worked around the roots of the plants, spreading nutrients and planting more seeds.

A new balance of life circled Turr, one that rose out of a need for change. Where once Turr had feared change, now she breathed in sync with it, feeling the laughter and joy of each creature living a life they'd chosen for themselves, rather than one chosen for them.

No longer did it matter how one was born or the shape of their body. Everyone had a purpose on Turr, all bringing life and joy to each other without a single one feeling left out or restricted.

Laughter burst forth beneath a fungus tree and filled the air with joy—a sound that carried life itself as it hovered around an adult shroomperson chasing a small sea of shroombabies.

"You better run faster! I'm coming to get you!" Imitating big crashing noises, the shroomparent stomped after the little babies as they giggled and squealed, their couple-inch-tall legs barely able to keep up. A few of them toppled over, their headcaps bouncing against the soft moss.

One of the little pink-capped shroombabies jumped onto the shroomparent's leg, hugging it close. They looked up with wide yellow eyes. "Invidia?"

Invidia scooped up the little baby, cupping them gently in their hands. "What do you want to ask now, Tessa?"

Tessa laughed as the others came running back, quickly sitting at Invidia's feet. "Tell us about the humans, Dama. Tell us about how Turr brought us and the garden city back to life."

Invidia groaned as they sat down, feigning annoyance. "I almost regret telling you about it in the first place. You ask about it *so* often."

The babies whined and begged, but Turr sent a soft breeze to quiet them. Something else was happening today. Something they'd been waiting on for a long time.

Invidia felt the breeze on their face and looked up. A whisper they hadn't heard for almost a year tickled their ear.

"Invidia!" A bright voice broke through the air as another shroomperson joined them.

"Clyra!" Invidia stood and pulled them in for a hug. The shroombabies scattered around them, running off to cause mischief elsewhere. Invidia cupped Clyra's face, careful not to touch where their cap was still regrowing. "What's happening?" they asked, their life force humming in sync with Clyra, in sync with Turr.

Tears filled Clyra's eyes. "I—the—" Unable to finish, they simply shook their head and tugged on Invidia's hand.

"I'll be back!" Invidia called to their shroombabies.

The little ones had already disappeared, enjoying the trouble they could get into while their dama wasn't paying attention. Turr laughed at them, then moved along behind the grown shroompeople, humming with anticipation.

The two caves covered with Resley's vines came into view. Invidia gave space in their spirit for the grief that rose at the sight. The life sprouting within these reminders of death always made them emotional. But today, they sensed a new kind of life beginning. Without even looking inside, Invidia threw their arms around Clyra, laughing, crying, and dancing as they congratulated their friend.

Heart full of delight at their celebration, Turr moved into the cave, moving through the life of the vines and the beetles crawling across them. She looked down at the dark, moist compost where a large ring of pinkish-red mushrooms sprouted.

One stood among them, humming with the same unique life as the other Turrians outside. With a squeaky yawn, it opened its eyes, looking around at the breeze kissing and tickling its cheek.

"Welcome to the world, little shroom," Turr whispered. This was a shroombaby born of hope, of

life, of love, of proof that in time, not just the garden city would heal—they all would.

Turr retreated from Isagani, leaving behind the creatures who'd fought so hard for her life. Warm and full of healing and acceptance, she lay down to rest. Finally, she could exist in peace again, wrapping her children in life, love, and protection once more.

In finding each other, you have found me.
Through each other's eyes you learned to see,
The answers I gave you through memories.
Then in healing each other, you have healed me.

ACKNOWLEDGEMENTS

Effie Joe's Acknowledgements:

Human Scars on Planet Skin isn't just about a living planet, it's a living story in and of itself. It lives on in our souls and emotions, in the way we process our grief, love, hope, and hopelessness. It's alive in Mother Earth, who I must thank firstly before anything else. For providing for us humans, giving us fresh water to drink, plants and animals to eat and tend, homes carved out of her bones of rock and metal, and for the tender embrace of dirt to dirt once we die. For taking care of us like Turr cares for her children.

And of course, the biggest hug and thank you goes next to Nathaniel, for brainstorming this book with me as a crazy idea we thought would never happen. For writing it in a mad scramble in less than two months, then letting it sit and stew for over half a year as we grew as people and became authors worthy of telling its story. For being a close companion and sitting with the raw emotion and vulnerability this book has created inside us. For holding my hand as we struggled through it together. For always pulling his weight and more in our work together. Thank you for being the best friend and co-author anyone could ask for.

Thank you to the growing community of readers we've found through Instagram who, like us, desire books that have outgrown the trends of modern society, that threaten to rip from our hearts, deep bloody emotions with plant-like hands. Thank you to Bethany Meyer and Stephanie Dunn for beta reading parts of this book, taking it all in and hyping us up before it'd become something actually worthy of the excitement. And for people like Judy Liu, Jessica Erdmann, and Kate Lawhon whose enthusiasm and obsession with this book helped keep me going.

Couldn't be more thrilled to have had Samantha Mendell's editing touch upon this book, ensuring I never have to worry about mean little typos haunting me months down the road.

Before we get to the end, I have to thank the incredible botanical and body horror authors who've come before us and inspired this book, chief of which are CG Drews, author of *Don't Let the Forest In*, and Noah Medlock, author of *A Botanical Daughter*. Thank you for planting the way before us.

And lastly, thank you, reader. For letting us take you along this journey, to the prettiest, most horrific places in Turr and in our hearts. I hope this book holds you softly and dearly in its leafy embrace.

—*Effie Joe Stock*

Nathaniel's Acknowledgments:

Standing on the other side of creating this story is so incredibly freeing. I'm grateful that I'm in the space where I'm able to pursue such unique ideas. This is the type of book I always wanted to write, but I'm not sure I would've had the courage or capability if I hadn't had a partner for it.

So first I have to thank Effie for writing this book with me. This story changed a lot during the writing process, and I like to think that we changed with it. Thank you for being the person who's willing to break genre expectations and craft something wholly unique. I can't believe we managed to pull this off, from the first day where we wrote a prologue to the final day where we suddenly had a whole novel draft.

I also have to give a huge shoutout to all the people who have stayed excited during the two years it took for us to get this book written and published. My siblings, my friends, people online who heard about it and desperately wanted it . . . all of you have helped more than you know.

Lastly, to the reader who's reading these words right now. A book can only make an impact if people are willing to read it. Thank you for reading this one.

—Nathaniel Luscombe

KICKSTARTER BACKERS

Huge thanks to every reader who put their money and hopes into this book by backing our Kickstarter:

Jess Autiero, Anya Amore, Anna B, Aimee B, Nikkita Bell, Niki Block, David Bock, Hannah Bodio, The Moirae Sisters Booktique!, Maria Bossard, Brandi, Victoria Buckland, Elizabeth N. Carrillo, Cheryl, Shonda Chrissonberry, Margaret Claire, Chiara Cooper, Kathleen Contine, Joyce Crane, Jessica Erdmann, Andrew Euston, Zack Fissel, Annie Fuller, Sarah Goehrke, Olivia Gratehouse, Trinh Ha, Abigail Hawthorne, Jeremy Hayes, Lisa Herrick, Adrienne Hood, Jess Instone, Jeanett, Alicia K, Nathan Kahl, Sergey Kochergan, KonvinnaS, Antal Kovács, Micha Kuhlemann, Kate Lawhon, Lex, Anke Liedbruster, Judy Liu, DrJaManita, Zachary Maxon, Emily May, Chase McGlinchey, Samantha Mendell, Jai Mohan, Sonia Munoz, Shelby Musante, Jace Nguyen, Evan Peck, Kyle Rey, Rheannon, RoRo, Monty K. Rue, Erica Rue, Orlinda Ruiz, Sabie, Anie Sallis, Nicole Sanborn, Sera, Rayleigh Setser, Skye Sisk, M.T. Solomon, R. Squat, Stosh, Elleigh Straight, George Titsworth, Frances Torres, Ness Vaughan, Marissa Villalobos, Kaitlyn Waggoner, K. Weikel, Matt Whetsell, Sara Wing, Jen Woodrum, Aingeal-Wroth, Sadie A Young, Dongyi Zhuyan, Micah & Ziel

ABOUT THE AUTHORS

EFFIE JOE STOCK is the author of The Shadows of Light series, creator of the world Rasa, and head of Dragon Bone Publishing. When she's not slaving away in front of her computer, you can find her playing music, studying psychology, theology, or philosophy, playing fantasy RPG video games, riding motorcycles, or hanging out with her farm animals. Her publishing journey only just beginning, Stock looks forward to the release of the rest of her fantasy series along with other Dragon Bone titles.

Website: www.effiejoestock.com
Instagram: @effie.joe.stock.author
YouTube: Effie Joe Stock

NATHANIEL LUSCOMBE is an author and publisher from Ontario, Canada. He's known for his existential writing, fun mashups of speculative genres, and making everything cozy (even horror). His most popular work is his science-fantasy novella *Moon Soul*. When he's not writing, he's busy co-running Dragon Bone Publishing and Dragon Heart Press.

Website: nathanielluscombe.com
Instagram: @nathaniel.luscombe
TikTok: @nathaniel.luscombe

MORE BY
DRAGON BONE PUBLISHING

FANTASY

THE RASAVERSE
The Legends of Rasa Vol. I
Child of the Dragon Prophecy
Heir of Two Kingdoms
Son of the Prophet

Bleached Reminders

SCIFI/SCIENCE FANTASY

Moon Soul
The Planets We Become

POETRY

When One World Ends, Another Begins
Tending Clay; Unearthing Stars
Best Cat in Show
ThistleHeart Home

CHILDREN'S LITERATURE

Turklet, Squeaky, and the Seven Chicken Chicks

ANTHOLOGIES

Aphotic Love
Unconventional Love
Unleash the Cosmos
The Dragon Bone Journal

Find Other Titles like *Human Scars on Planet Skin* at:
www.dragonbonepublishing.com